World's Best Short Stories

BESTSELLING FICTION

- 1984 by George Orwell
  Fiction/Classics, ISBN: 9788193545836
- Animal Farm by George Orwell
  Fiction/Classics, ISBN: 9789387669062
- Anthem by Ayn Rand
  Fiction/Classics, ISBN: 9789389157178
- As a Man Thinketh by James Allen
  Fiction/Classics, ISBN: 9789388118422
- Demian by Hermann Hesse
  Fiction/Classics, ISBN: 9789388118170
- Gitanjali by Rabindranath Tagore
  Fiction/Poems, ISBN: 9789387669079
- Mansarover 1 (Hindi) by Premchand
  Fiction/Short Stories, ISBN: 9789387669086
- Selected Stories of Rabindranath Tagore by Tagore
  Fiction/Short Stories, ISBN: 9789387669307
- Siddhartha by Hermann Hesse
  Fiction/Classics, ISBN: 9789387669116
- Tales from India by Rudyard Kipling
  Fiction/Short Stories, ISBN: 9789387669123
- Tales from Shakespeare by Charles Lamb, Mary Lamb
  Fiction/Short Stories, ISBN: 9789387669314
- The Jungle Book by Rudyard Kipling
  Children's/Classics, ISBN: 9789387669338
- The Light of Asia by Sir Edwin Arnold
  Fiction/Poetry, ISBN: 9789387669130
- The Prophet by Kahlil Gibran
  Fiction/Classics, ISBN: 9789388118453

Search the book by its ISBN

1

WORLD'S BEST SHORT STORIES

GP EDITORS

GENERAL PRESS

Published by

GENERAL PRESS

4805/24, Fourth Floor, Krishna House
Ansari Road, Daryaganj, New Delhi - 110002
Ph : 011-23282971, 45795759
E-mail : generalpressindia@gmail.com

www.generalpress.in

First Edition : 2022

ISBN : 9789354990885

Published by Azeem Ahmad Khan for General Press

Contents

Story 1

THE DEATH OF A CLERK

Anton Chekhov

One fine evening, a no less fine government clerk called Ivan Dmitritch Tchervyakov was sitting in the second row of the stalls, gazing through an opera glass at the *Cloches de Corneville*. He gazed and felt at the acme of bliss. But suddenly… In stories one so often meets with this "But suddenly." The authors are right: life is so full of surprises! But suddenly his face puckered up, his eyes disappeared, his breathing was arrested … he took the opera glass from his eyes, bent over and … "Aptchee!!" he sneezed as you perceive. It is not reprehensible for anyone to sneeze anywhere. Peasants sneeze and so do police superintendents, and sometimes even privy councillors. All men sneeze. Tchervyakov was not in the least confused, he wiped his face with his handkerchief, and like a polite man, looked round to see whether he had disturbed any one by his sneezing. But then he was overcome with confusion. He saw that an old gentleman sitting in front of him in the first row of the stalls was carefully wiping his bald head and his neck with his glove and muttering something to himself. In the old gentleman, Tchervyakov recognised Brizzhalov, a civilian general serving in the Department of Transport.

"I have spattered him," thought Tchervyakov, "he is not the head of my department, but still it is awkward. I must apologise."

Tchervyakov gave a cough, bent his whole person forward, and whispered in the general's ear.

"Pardon, your Excellency, I spattered you accidentally..."

"Never mind, never mind."

"For goodness sake excuse me, I ... I did not mean to."

"Oh, please, sit down! Let me listen!"

Tchervyakov was embarrassed, he smiled stupidly and fell to gazing at the stage. He gazed at it but was no longer feeling bliss. He began to be troubled by uneasiness. In the interval, he went up to Brizzhalov, walked beside him, and overcoming his shyness, muttered:

"I spattered you, your Excellency, forgive me ... you see ... I didn't do it to ..."

"Oh, that's enough ... I'd forgotten it, and you keep on about it!" said the general, moving his lower lip impatiently.

"He has forgotten, but there is a fiendish light in his eye," thought Tchervyakov, looking suspiciously at the general. "And he doesn't want to talk. I ought to explain to him ... that I really didn't intend ... that it is the law of nature or else he will think I meant to spit on him. He doesn't think so now, but he will think so later!"

On getting home, Tchervyakov told his wife of his breach of good manners. It struck him that his wife took too frivolous a view of the incident; she was a little frightened, but when she learned that Brizzhalov was in a different department, she was reassured.

"Still, you had better go and apologise," she said, "or he will think you don't know how to behave in public."

"That's just it! I did apologise, but he took it somehow queerly … he didn't say a word of sense. There wasn't time to talk properly."

Next day Tchervyakov put on a new uniform, had his hair cut and went to Brizzhalov's to explain; going into the general's reception room he saw there a number of petitioners and among them the general himself, who was beginning to interview them. After questioning several petitioners the general raised his eyes and looked at Tchervyakov.

"Yesterday at the *Arcadia*, if you recollect, your Excellency," the latter began, "I sneezed and … accidentally spattered … Exc…"

"What nonsense… It's beyond anything! What can I do for you," said the general addressing the next petitioner.

"He won't speak," thought Tchervyakov, turning pale; "that means that he is angry… No, it can't be left like this… I will explain to him."

When the general had finished his conversation with the last of the petitioners and was turning towards his inner apartments, Tchervyakov took a step towards him and muttered:

"Your Excellency! If I venture to trouble your Excellency, it is simply from a feeling I may say of regret! ... It was not intentional if you will graciously believe me."

The general made a lachrymose face, and waved his hand.

"Why, you are simply making fun of me, sir," he said as he closed the door behind him.

"Where's the making fun in it?" thought Tchervyakov, "there is nothing of the sort! He is a general, but he can't understand. If that is how it is I am not going to apologise to that *fanfaron* any more! The devil take him. I'll write a letter to him, but I won't go. By Jove, I won't."

So thought Tchervyakov as he walked home; he did not write a letter to the general, he pondered and pondered and could not make up that letter. He had to go next day to explain in person.

"I ventured to disturb your Excellency yesterday," he muttered, when the general lifted enquiring eyes upon him, "not to make fun as you were pleased to say. I was apologising for having spattered you in sneezing... And I did not dream of making fun of you. Should I dare to make fun of you, if we should take to making fun, then there would be no respect for persons, there would be..."

"Be off!" yelled the general, turning suddenly purple, and shaking all over.

"What?" asked Tchervyakov, in a whisper turning numb with horror.

"Be off!" repeated the general, stamping.

Something seemed to give way in Tchervyakov's stomach. Seeing nothing and hearing nothing he reeled to the door, went out into the street, and went staggering along… Reaching home mechanically, without taking off his uniform, he lay down on the sofa and died.

STORY 2

A SCANDAL IN BOHEMIA

Sir Arthur Conan Doyle

1

To Sherlock Holmes she is always *the* woman. I have seldom heard him mention her under any other name. In his eyes she eclipses and predominates the whole of her sex. It was not that he felt any emotion akin to love for Irene Adler. All emotions, and that one particularly, were abhorrent to his cold, precise but admirably balanced mind. He was, I take it, the most perfect reasoning and observing machine that the world has seen, but as a lover he would have placed himself in a false position. He never spoke of the softer passions, save with a gibe and a sneer. They were admirable things for the observer—excellent for drawing the veil from men's motives and actions. But for the trained reasoner to admit such intrusions into his own delicate and finely adjusted temperament was to introduce a distracting factor which might throw a doubt upon all his mental results. Grit in a sensitive instrument, or a crack in one of his own high-power lenses, would not be more disturbing than a strong emotion in a nature such as his. And yet there was but one woman to him, and that woman was the late Irene Adler, of dubious and questionable memory.

I had seen little of Holmes lately. My marriage had drifted us away from each other. My own complete happiness, and the home-centred interests which rise up around the man who first finds himself master of his own establishment, were sufficient to absorb all my attention, while Holmes, who loathed every form of society with his whole Bohemian soul, remained in our lodgings in Baker Street, buried among his old books, and alternating from week to week between cocaine and ambition, the drowsiness of the drug, and the fierce energy of his own keen nature. He was still, as ever, deeply attracted by the study of crime, and occupied his immense faculties and extraordinary powers of observation in following out those clues, and clearing up those mysteries which had been abandoned as hopeless by the official police. From time to time I heard some vague account of his doings: of his summons to Odessa in the case of the Trepoff murder, of his clearing up of the singular tragedy of the Atkinson brothers at Trincomalee, and finally of the mission which he had accomplished so delicately and successfully for the reigning family of Holland. Beyond these signs of his activity, however, which I merely shared with all the readers of the daily press, I knew little of my former friend and companion.

One night—it was on the twentieth of March, 1888—I was returning from a journey to a patient (for I had now returned to civil practice), when my way led me through

Baker Street. As I passed the well-remembered door, which must always be associated in my mind with my wooing, and with the dark incidents of the Study in Scarlet, I was seized with a keen desire to see Holmes again, and to know how he was employing his extraordinary powers. His rooms were brilliantly lit, and, even as I looked up, I saw his tall, spare figure pass twice in a dark silhouette against the blind. He was pacing the room swiftly, eagerly, with his head sunk upon his chest and his hands clasped behind him. To me, who knew his every mood and habit, his attitude and manner told their own story. He was at work again. He had risen out of his drug-created dreams and was hot upon the scent of some new problem. I rang the bell and was shown up to the chamber which had formerly been in part my own.

His manner was not effusive. It seldom was; but he was glad, I think, to see me. With hardly a word spoken, but with a kindly eye, he waved me to an armchair, threw across his case of cigars, and indicated a spirit case and a gasogene in the corner. Then he stood before the fire and looked me over in his singular introspective fashion.

"Wedlock suits you," he remarked. "I think, Watson, that you have put on seven and a half pounds since I saw you."

"Seven!" I answered.

"Indeed, I should have thought a little more. Just a trifle more, I fancy, Watson. And in practice again, I observe. You did not tell me that you intended to go into harness."

"Then, how do you know?"

"I see it, I deduce it. How do I know that you have been getting yourself very wet lately, and that you have a most clumsy and careless servant girl?"

"My dear Holmes," said I, "This is too much. You would certainly have been burned, had you lived a few centuries ago. It is true that I had a country walk on Thursday and came home in a dreadful mess, but as I have changed my clothes I can't imagine how you deduce it. As to Mary Jane, she is incorrigible, and my wife has given her notice, but there, again, I fail to see how you work it out."

He chuckled to himself and rubbed his long, nervous hands together.

"It is simplicity itself," said he; "My eyes tell me that on the inside of your left shoe, just where the firelight strikes it, the leather is scored by six almost parallel cuts. Obviously they have been caused by someone who has very carelessly scraped round the edges of the sole in order to remove crusted mud from it. Hence, you see, my double deduction that you had been out in vile weather, and that you had a particularly malignant boot-slitting specimen of the London slavery. As to your practice, if a gentleman walks into my rooms smelling of iodoform, with a black mark of nitrate of silver upon his right forefinger, and a bulge on the right side of his top-hat to show where he has secreted his stethoscope, I must be dull, indeed, if I do not pronounce him to be an active member of the medical profession."

I could not help laughing at the ease with which he explained his process of deduction. "When I hear you give your reasons," I remarked, "The thing always appears to me to be so ridiculously simple that I could easily do it myself, though at each successive instance of your reasoning I am baffled until you explain your process. And yet I believe that my eyes are as good as yours."

"Quite so," he answered, lighting a cigarette, and throwing himself down into an armchair. "You see, but you do not observe. The distinction is clear. For example, you have frequently seen the steps which lead up from the hall to this room."

"Frequently."

"How often?"

"Well, some hundreds of times."

"Then how many are there?"

"How many? I don't know."

"Quite so! You have not observed. And yet you have seen. That is just my point. Now, I know that there are seventeen steps, because I have both seen and observed. By-the-way, since you are interested in these little problems, and since you are good enough to chronicle one or two of my trifling experiences, you may be interested in this." He threw over a sheet of thick, pink-tinted note-paper which had been lying open upon the table. "It came by the last post," said he. "Read it aloud."

The note was undated, and without either signature or address.

> "There will call upon you tonight, at a quarter to eight o'clock," it said, "A gentleman who desires to consult you upon a matter of the very deepest moment. Your recent services to one of the royal houses of Europe have shown that you are one who may safely be trusted with matters which are of an importance which can

hardly be exaggerated. This account of you we have from all quarters received. Be in your chamber then at that hour, and do not take it amiss if your visitor wear a mask."

"This is indeed a mystery," I remarked. "What do you imagine that it means?"

"I have no data yet. It is a capital mistake to theorize before one has data. Insensibly one begins to twist facts to suit theories, instead of theories to suit facts. But the note itself. What do you deduce from it?"

I carefully examined the writing, and the paper upon which it was written.

"The man who wrote it was presumably well to do," I remarked, endeavouring to imitate my companion's processes. "Such paper could not be bought under half a crown a packet. It is peculiarly strong and stiff."

"Peculiar—that is the very word," said Holmes. "It is not an English paper at all. Hold it up to the light."

I did so, and saw a large "E" with a small "g," a "P," and a large "G" with a small "t" woven into the texture of the paper.

"What do you make of that?" asked Holmes.

"The name of the maker, no doubt; or his monogram, rather."

"Not at all. The 'G' with the small 't' stands for 'Gesellschaft,' which is the German for 'Company.' It is a customary contraction like our 'Co.' '*P*,' of course, stands for 'Papier.' Now for the '*Eg*.' Let us glance at our Continental Gazetteer." He took down a heavy brown volume from his shelves. "Eglow, Eglonitz—here we are, Egria. It is in a German-speaking country—in Bohemia, not far from Carlsbad. 'Remarkable as being the scene of the death of Wallenstein, and for its numerous glass-factories and paper-mills." Ha, ha, my boy, what do you make of that?" His eyes sparkled, and he sent up a great blue triumphant cloud from his cigarette.

"The paper was made in Bohemia," I said.

"Precisely. And the man who wrote the note is a German. Do you note the peculiar construction of the sentence—'This account of you we have from all quarters received.' A Frenchman or Russian could not have written that. It is the German who is so uncourteous to his verbs. It only remains, therefore, to discover what is wanted by this German who writes upon Bohemian paper and prefers wearing a mask to showing his face. And here he comes, if I am not mistaken, to resolve all our doubts."

As he spoke there was the sharp sound of horses' hoofs and grating wheels against the curb, followed by a sharp pull at the bell. Holmes whistled.

"A pair, by the sound," said he. "Yes," he continued, glancing out of the window. "A nice little brougham and a pair of beauties. A hundred and fifty guineas apiece. There's money in this case, Watson, if there is nothing else."

"I think that I had better go, Holmes."

"Not a bit, Doctor. Stay where you are. I am lost without my Boswell. And this promises to be interesting. It would be a pity to miss it."

"But your client—"

"Never mind him. I may want your help, and so may he. Here he comes. Sit down in that armchair, Doctor, and give us your best attention."

A slow and heavy step, which had been heard upon the stairs and in the passage, paused immediately outside the door. Then there was a loud and authoritative tap.

"Come in!" said Holmes.

A man entered who could hardly have been less than six feet six inches in height, with the chest and limbs of a Hercules. His dress was rich with a richness which would, in England, be looked upon as akin to bad taste. Heavy bands of astrakhan were slashed across the sleeves and fronts of his double-breasted coat, while the deep blue cloak which was thrown over his shoulders was lined with flame-coloured silk and secured at the neck with a brooch which consisted of a single flaming beryl. Boots which extended halfway up his calves, and which were trimmed at the tops with rich brown fur, completed the impression of barbaric opulence which was suggested by his whole appearance. He carried a broad-brimmed hat in his hand, while he wore across the upper part of his face, extending down past the cheekbones, a black vizard mask, which he had apparently adjusted that very moment, for his hand was still raised to it as he entered. From the lower part of the face he appeared to be a man of strong character, with a thick, hanging lip, and a long, straight chin suggestive of resolution pushed to the length of obstinacy.

"You had my note?" he asked with a deep harsh voice and a strongly marked German accent. "I told you that I would call." He looked from one to the other of us, as if uncertain which to address.

"Pray take a seat," said Holmes. "This is my friend and colleague, Dr. Watson, who is occasionally good enough to help me in my cases. Whom have I the honour to address?"

"You may address me as the Count Von Kramm, a Bohemian nobleman. I understand that this gentleman, your friend, is a man of honour and discretion, whom I may trust with a matter of the most extreme importance. If not, I should much prefer to communicate with you alone."

I rose to go, but Holmes caught me by the wrist and pushed me back into my chair. "It is both, or none," said he. "You may say before this gentleman anything which you may say to me."

The Count shrugged his broad shoulders. "Then I must begin," said he, "by binding you both to absolute secrecy for two years; at the end of that time the matter will be of no importance. At present it is not too much to say that it is of such weight it may have an influence upon European history."

"I promise," said Holmes.

"And I."

"You will excuse this mask," continued our strange visitor. "The august person who employs me wishes his agent to be unknown to you, and I may confess at once that the title by which I have just called myself is not exactly my own."

"I was aware of it," said Holmes dryly.

"The circumstances are of great delicacy, and every precaution has to be taken to quench what might grow to be an immense scandal and seriously compromise one of the reigning families of Europe. To speak plainly, the matter implicates the great House of Ormstein, hereditary kings of Bohemia."

"I was also aware of that," murmured Holmes, settling himself down in his armchair and closing his eyes.

Our visitor glanced with some apparent surprise at the languid, lounging figure of the man who had been no doubt depicted to him as the most incisive reasoner and most energetic agent in Europe. Holmes slowly reopened his eyes and looked impatiently at his gigantic client.

"If your Majesty would condescend to state your case," he remarked, "I should be better able to advise you."

The man sprang from his chair and paced up and down the room in uncontrollable agitation. Then, with a gesture of desperation, he tore the mask from his face and hurled it upon the ground. "You are right," he cried; "I am the King. Why should I attempt to conceal it?"

"Why, indeed?" murmured Holmes. "Your Majesty had not spoken before I was aware that I was addressing Wilhelm Gottsreich Sigismond von Ormstein, Grand Duke of Cassel-Felstein, and hereditary King of Bohemia."

"But you can understand," said our strange visitor, sitting down once more and passing his hand over his high white forehead, "you can understand that I am not accustomed to doing such business in my own person. Yet the matter was so delicate that I could not confide it to an agent without putting myself in his power. I have come incognito from Prague for the purpose of consulting you."

"Then, pray consult," said Holmes, shutting his eyes once more.

"The facts are briefly these: Some five years ago, during a lengthy visit to Warsaw, I made the acquaintance of the well-known adventuress, Irene Adler. The name is no doubt familiar to you."

"Kindly look her up in my index, Doctor," murmured Holmes without opening his eyes. For many years he had adopted a system of docketing all paragraphs concerning men and things, so that it was difficult to name a subject or a person on which he could not at once furnish information. In this case I found her biography sandwiched in between that of a Hebrew rabbi and that of a staff-commander who had written a monograph upon the deep-sea fishes.

"Let me see!" said Holmes. "Hum! Born in New Jersey in the year 1858. Contralto—hum! La Scala, hum! Prima donna Imperial Opera of Warsaw—yes! Retired from operatic stage—ha! Living in London—quite so! Your Majesty, as I understand, became entangled with this young person, wrote her some compromising letters, and is now desirous of getting those letters back."

"Precisely so. But how—"

"Was there a secret marriage?"

"None."

"No legal papers or certificates?"

"None."

"Then I fail to follow your Majesty. If this young person should produce her letters for blackmailing or other purposes, how is she to prove their authenticity?"

"There is the writing."

"Pooh, pooh! Forgery."

"My private note-paper."

"Stolen."

"My own seal."

"Imitated."

"My photograph."

"Bought."

"We were both in the photograph."

"Oh, dear! That is very bad! Your Majesty has indeed committed an indiscretion."

"I was mad—insane."

"You have compromised yourself seriously."

"I was only Crown Prince then. I was young. I am but thirty now."

"It must be recovered."

"We have tried and failed."

"Your Majesty must pay. It must be bought."

"She will not sell."

"Stolen, then."

"Five attempts have been made. Twice burglars in my pay ransacked her house. Once we diverted her luggage when she travelled. Twice she has been waylaid. There has been no result."

"No sign of it?"

"Absolutely none."

Holmes laughed. "It is quite a pretty little problem," said he.

"But a very serious one to me," returned the King reproachfully.

"Very, indeed. And what does she propose to do with the photograph?"

"To ruin me."

"But how?"

"I am about to be married."

"So I have heard."

"To Clotilde Lothman von Saxe-Meningen, second daughter of the King of Scandinavia. You may know the strict principles of her family. She is herself the very soul of delicacy. A shadow of a doubt as to my conduct would bring the matter to an end."

"And Irene Adler?"

"Threatens to send them the photograph. And she will do it. I know that she will do it. You do not know her, but she has a soul of steel. She has the face of the most beautiful of women, and the mind of the most resolute of men. Rather than I should marry another woman, there are no lengths to which she would not go—none."

"You are sure that she has not sent it yet?"

"I am sure."

"And why?"

"Because she has said that she would send it on the day when the betrothal was publicly proclaimed. That will be next Monday."

"Oh, then we have three days yet," said Holmes with a yawn. "That is very fortunate, as I have one or two matters of importance to look into just at present. Your Majesty will, of course, stay in London for the present?"

"Certainly. You will find me at the Langham under the name of the Count Von Kramm."

"Then I shall drop you a line to let you know how we progress."

"Pray do so. I shall be all anxiety."

"Then, as to money?"

"You have carte blanche."

"Absolutely?"

"I tell you that I would give one of the provinces of my kingdom to have that photograph."

"And for present expenses?"

The King took a heavy chamois leather bag from under his cloak and laid it on the table.

"There are three hundred pounds in gold and seven hundred in notes," he said.

Holmes scribbled a receipt upon a sheet of his note-book and handed it to him.

"And Mademoiselle's address?" he asked.

"Is Briony Lodge, Serpentine Avenue, St. John's Wood."

Holmes took a note of it. "One other question," said he. "Was the photograph a cabinet?"

"It was."

"Then, good-night, your Majesty, and I trust that we shall soon have some good news for you. And good-night, Watson," he added, as the wheels of the royal brougham rolled down the street. "If you will be good enough to call tomorrow afternoon at three o'clock I should like to chat this little matter over with you."

2

At three o'clock precisely I was at Baker Street, but Holmes had not yet returned. The landlady informed me that he had left the house shortly after eight o'clock in the morning. I sat down beside the fire, however, with the intention of awaiting him, however long he might be. I was already deeply interested in his inquiry, for, though it was surrounded by none of the grim and strange features which were associated with the two crimes which I have already recorded, still, the nature of the case and the exalted station of his client gave it a character of its own. Indeed, apart from the nature of the investigation which my friend had on hand, there was something in his masterly grasp of a situation, and his keen, incisive reasoning, which made it a pleasure to me to study his system of work, and to follow the quick, subtle methods by which he disentangled the most inextricable mysteries. So accustomed was I to his invariable success that the very possibility of his failing had ceased to enter into my head.

It was close upon four before the door opened, and a drunken-looking groom, ill-kempt and side-whiskered, with an inflamed face and disreputable clothes, walked into the room. Accustomed as I was to my friend's amazing powers in the use of disguises, I had to look three times before I was certain that it was indeed he. With a nod he vanished into the bedroom, whence he emerged in five minutes tweed-suited and respectable, as of old. Putting his hands into his pockets, he stretched out his legs in front of the fire and laughed heartily for some minutes.

"Well, really!" he cried, and then he choked and laughed again until he was obliged to lie back, limp and helpless, in the chair.

"What is it?"

"It's quite too funny. I am sure you could never guess how I employed my morning, or what I ended by doing."

"I can't imagine. I suppose that you have been watching the habits, and perhaps the house, of Miss Irene Adler."

"Quite so; but the sequel was rather unusual. I will tell you, however. I left the house a little after eight o'clock this morning in the character of a groom out of work. There is a wonderful sympathy and freemasonry among horsey men. Be one of them, and you will know all that there is to know. I soon found Briony Lodge. It is a *bijou* villa, with a garden at the back, but built out in front right up to the road, two stories. Chubb lock to the door. Large sitting-room on the right side, well furnished, with long windows almost to the floor, and those preposterous English window fasteners which a child could open. Behind there was nothing remarkable, save that the passage window could be reached from the top of the coach-house. I walked round it and examined it closely from every point of view, but without noting anything else of interest.

"I then lounged down the street and found, as I expected, that there was a mews in a lane which runs down by one wall of the garden. I lent the ostlers a hand in rubbing down their horses, and received in exchange two pence, a glass of half and half, two fills of shag tobacco, and as much information as I could desire about Miss Adler, to say nothing of half a dozen other people in the neighbourhood in whom I was not in the least interested, but whose biographies I was compelled to listen to."

"And what of Irene Adler?" I asked.

"Oh, she has turned all the men's heads down in that part. She is the daintiest thing under a bonnet on this planet. So say the Serpentine-mews, to a man. She lives quietly, sings at concerts, drives out at five every day, and returns at seven sharp for dinner. Seldom goes out at other times, except when she sings. Has only one male visitor, but a good deal of him. He is dark, handsome, and dashing, never calls less than once a day, and often twice. He is a Mr. Godfrey Norton, of the Inner Temple. See the advantages of a cabman as a confidant. They had driven him home a dozen times from Serpentine-mews, and knew all about him. When I had listened to all they had to tell, I began to walk up and down near Briony Lodge once more, and to think over my plan of campaign.

"This Godfrey Norton was evidently an important factor in the matter. He was a lawyer. That sounded ominous. What was the relation between them, and what the object of his repeated visits? Was she his client, his friend, or his mistress? If the former, she had probably transferred the photograph to his keeping. If the latter, it was less likely. On the issue of this question depended whether I should continue my work at Briony Lodge, or turn my attention to the gentleman's chambers in the Temple. It was a delicate point, and it widened the field of my inquiry. I fear that I bore you with these details, but I have to let you see my little difficulties, if you are to understand the situation."

"I am following you closely," I answered.

"I was still balancing the matter in my mind when a handsome cab drove up to Briony Lodge, and a gentleman sprang out. He was a remarkably handsome man, dark, aquiline, and moustached—evidently the man of whom I had heard. He appeared to be in a great hurry, shouted to the cabman to wait, and brushed past the maid who opened the door with the air of a man who was thoroughly at home.

"He was in the house about half an hour, and I could catch glimpses of him in the windows of the sitting-room, pacing up and down, talking excitedly, and waving his arms. Of her I could see nothing. Presently he emerged, looking even more flurried than before. As he stepped up to the cab, he pulled a gold watch from his pocket and looked at it earnestly, 'Drive like the devil,' he shouted, 'first to Gross & Hankey's in Regent Street, and then to the Church of St. Monica in the Edgeware Road. Half a guinea if you do it in twenty minutes!'

"Away they went, and I was just wondering whether I should not do well to follow them when up the lane come a neat little landau, the coachman with his coat only half-buttoned, and his tie under his ear, while all the tags of his harness were sticking out of the buckles. It hadn't pulled up before she shot out of the hall door and into it. I only caught a glimpse of her at the moment, but she was a lovely woman, with a face that a man might die for.

" 'The Church of St. Monica, John,' she cried, 'and half a sovereign if you reach it in twenty minutes.'

"This was quite too good to lose, Watson. I was just balancing whether I should run for it, or whether I should perch behind her landau when a cab came through the street. The driver looked twice at such a shabby fare, but I jumped in before he could object. 'The Church of St. Monica,' said I, 'and half a sovereign if you reach it in twenty minutes.' It was twenty-five minutes to twelve, and of course it was clear enough what was in the wind.

"My cabby drove fast. I don't think I ever drove faster, but the others were there before us. The cab and the landau with their steaming horses were in front of the door when I arrived. I paid the man and hurried into the church. There was not a soul there save the two whom I had followed and a surpliced clergyman, who seemed to be expostulating with them. They were all three standing in a knot in front of the altar. I lounged up the side aisle like any other idler who has dropped into a church. Suddenly, to my surprise, the three at the altar faced round to me, and Godfrey Norton came running as hard as he could towards me.

" 'Thank God,' he cried. 'You'll do. Come! Come!'

" 'What then?' I asked.

" 'Come, man, come, only three minutes, or it won't be legal.'

"I was half-dragged up to the altar, and before I knew where I was I found myself mumbling responses which were whispered in my ear, and vouching for things of which I knew nothing, and generally assisting in the secure tying up of Irene Adler, spinster, to Godfrey Norton, bachelor. It was all done in an instant, and there was the gentleman thanking me on the one side and the lady on the other, while the clergyman beamed on me in front. It was the most preposterous position in which I ever found myself in my life, and it was the thought of it that started me laughing just now. It seems that there had been some informality about their license, that the clergyman absolutely refused to marry them without a witness of some sort, and that my lucky appearance saved the bridegroom from having to sally out into the streets in search of a best man. The bride gave me a sovereign, and I mean to wear it on my watch-chain in memory of the occasion."

"This is a much unexpected turn of affairs," said I; "and what then?"

"Well, I found my plans very seriously menaced. It looked as if the pair might take an immediate departure, and so necessitate very prompt and energetic measures on my part. At the church door, however, they separated, he driving back to the Temple, and she to her own house. 'I shall drive out in the park at five as usual,' she said as she left him. I heard no more. They drove away in different directions, and I went off to make my own arrangements."

"Which are?"

"Some cold beef and a glass of beer," he answered, ringing the bell. "I have been too busy to think of food, and I am likely to be busier still this evening. By the way, Doctor, I shall want your co-operation."

"I shall be delighted."

"You don't mind breaking the law?"

"Not in the least."

"Nor running a chance of arrest?"

"Not in a good cause."

"Oh, the cause is excellent!"

"Then I am your man."

"I was sure that I might rely on you."

"But what is it you wish?"

"When Mrs. Turner has brought in the tray I will make it clear to you. Now," he said as he turned hungrily on the simple fare that our landlady had provided, "I must discuss it while I eat, for I have not much time. It is nearly five now. In two hours we must be on the scene of action. Miss Irene, or Madame, rather, returns from her drive at seven. We must be at Briony Lodge to meet her."

"And what then?"

"You must leave that to me. I have already arranged what is to occur. There is only one point on which I must insist. You must not interfere, come what may. You understand?"

"I am to be neutral?"

"To do nothing whatever. There will probably be some small unpleasantness. Do not join in it. It will end in my being conveyed into the house. Four or five minutes afterwards the sitting-room window will open. You are to station yourself close to that open window."

"Yes."

"You are to watch me, for I will be visible to you."

"Yes."

"And when I raise my hand—so—you will throw into the room what I give you to throw, and will, at the same time, raise the cry of fire. You quite follow me?"

"Entirely."

"It is nothing very formidable," he said, taking a long cigar-shaped roll from his pocket. "It is an ordinary plumber's smoke-rocket, fitted with a cap at either end to make it self-lighting. Your task is confined to that. When you raise your cry of fire, it will be taken up by quite a number of people.

You may then walk to the end of the street, and I will rejoin you in ten minutes. I hope that I have made myself clear?"

"I am to remain neutral, to get near the window, to watch you, and at the signal to throw in this object, then to raise the cry of fire, and to wait you at the corner of the street."

"Precisely."

"Then you may entirely rely on me."

"That is excellent. I think, perhaps, it is almost time that I prepare for the new role I have to play."

He disappeared into his bedroom and returned in a few minutes in the character of an amiable and simple-minded Nonconformist clergyman. His broad black hat, his baggy trousers, his white tie, his sympathetic smile, and general look of peering and benevolent curiosity were such as Mr. John Hare alone could have equalled. It was not merely that Holmes changed his costume. His expression, his manner, his very soul seemed to vary with every fresh part that he assumed. The stage lost a fine actor, even as science lost an acute reasoner, when he became a specialist in crime.

It was a quarter past six when we left Baker Street, and it still wanted ten minutes to the hour when we found ourselves in Serpentine Avenue. It was already dusk, and the lamps were just being lighted as we paced up and down in front of Briony Lodge, waiting for the coming of its occupant. The house was just such as I had pictured it from Sherlock Holmes' succinct description, but the locality appeared to be less private than I expected. On the contrary, for a small street in a quiet neighbourhood, it was remarkably animated. There was a group of shabbily dressed men smoking and laughing in a corner, a scissors-grinder with his wheel, two guardsmen who were flirting with a nurse-girl, and several well-dressed young men who were lounging up and down with cigars in their mouths.

"You see," remarked Holmes, as we paced to and fro in front of the house, "This marriage rather simplifies matters. The photograph becomes a double-edged weapon now. The chances are that she would be as averse to its being seen by Mr. Godfrey Norton, as our client is to its coming to the eyes of his princess. Now the question is, Where are we to find the photograph?"

"Where, indeed?"

"It is most unlikely that she carries it about with her. It is cabinet size. Too large for easy concealment about a woman's dress. She knows that the King is capable of having her waylaid and searched. Two attempts of the sort have already been made. We may take it, then, that she does not carry it about with her."

"Where, then?"

"Her banker or her lawyer. There is that double possibility. But I am inclined to think neither. Women are naturally secretive, and they like to do their own secreting. Why should she hand it over to anyone else? She could trust her own guardianship, but she could not tell what indirect or political influence might be brought to bear upon a business man. Besides, remember that she had resolved to use it within a few days. It must be where she can lay her hands upon it. It must be in her own house."

"But it has twice been burgled."

"Pshaw! They did not know how to look."

"But how will you look?"

"I will not look."

"What then?"

"I will get her to show me."

"But she will refuse."

"She will not be able to. But I hear the rumble of wheels. It is her carriage. Now carry out my orders to the letter."

As he spoke the gleam of the side-lights of a carriage came round the curve of the avenue. It was a smart little landau which rattled up to the door of Briony Lodge. As it pulled up, one of the loafing men at the corner dashed forward to open the door in the hope of earning a copper, but was elbowed away by another loafer, who had rushed up with the same intention. A fierce quarrel broke out, which was increased by the two guardsmen, who took sides with one of the loungers, and by the scissors-grinder, who was equally hot upon the other side. A blow was struck, and in an instant the lady, who had stepped from her carriage, was the centre of a little knot of flushed and struggling men, who struck savagely at each other with their fists and sticks. Holmes dashed into the crowd to protect the lady; but just as he reached her he gave a cry and dropped to the ground, with the blood running freely down his face. At his fall the guardsmen took to their heels in one direction and the loungers in the other, while a number of better-dressed people, who had watched the scuffle without taking part in it, crowded in to help the lady and to attend to the injured man. Irene Adler, as I will still call her, had hurried up the steps; but she stood at the top with her superb figure outlined against the lights of the hall, looking back into the street.

"Is the poor gentleman much hurt?" she asked.

"He is dead," cried several voices.

"No, no, there's life in him!" shouted another. "But he'll be gone before you can get him to hospital."

"He's a brave fellow," said a woman. "They would have had the lady's purse and watch if it hadn't been for him. They were a gang, and a rough one, too. Ah, he's breathing now."

"He can't lie in the street. May we bring him in, marm?"

"Surely. Bring him into the sitting-room. There is a comfortable sofa. This way, please!"

Slowly and solemnly he was borne into Briony Lodge and laid out in the principal room, while I still observed the proceedings from my post by the window. The lamps had been lit, but the blinds had not been drawn, so that I could see Holmes as he lay upon the couch. I do not know whether he was seized with compunction at that moment for the part he was playing, but I know that I never felt more heartily ashamed of myself in my life than when I saw the beautiful creature against which I was conspiring or the grace and kindliness with which she waited upon the injured man. And yet it would be the blackest treachery to Holmes to draw back now from the part which he had intrusted to me. I hardened my heart, and took the smoke-rocket from under my ulster. After all, I thought, we are not injuring her. We are but preventing her from injuring another.

Holmes had sat up upon the couch, and I saw him motion like a man who is in need of air. A maid rushed across and threw open the window. At the same instant I saw him raise his hand and at the signal I tossed my rocket into the room with a cry of "Fire!" The word was no sooner out of my mouth than the whole crowd of spectators, well dressed and ill—gentlemen, ostlers, and servant-maids—joined in a general shriek of "Fire!" Thick clouds of smoke curled through the room and out at the open window. I caught a glimpse of rushing figures, and a moment later the voice of Holmes from within assuring them that it was a false alarm. Slipping through the shouting crowd I made my way to the corner of the street, and in ten minutes was rejoiced to find my friend's arm in mine, and to get away from the scene of uproar. He walked swiftly and in silence for some few minutes until we had turned down one of the quiet streets which lead towards the Edgeware Road.

"You did it very nicely, Doctor," he remarked. "Nothing could have been better. It is all right."

"You have the photograph?"

"I know where it is."

"And how did you find out?"

"She showed me, as I told you she would."

"I am still in the dark."

"I do not wish to make a mystery," said he, laughing. "The matter was perfectly simple. You, of course, saw that everyone in the street was an accomplice. They were all engaged for the evening."

"I guessed as much."

"Then, when the row broke out, I had a little moist red paint in the palm of my hand. I rushed forward, fell down, clapped my hand to my face, and became a piteous spectacle. It is an old trick."

"That also I could fathom."

"Then they carried me in. She was bound to have me in. What else could she do? And into her sitting-room, which was the very room which I suspected. It lay between that and her bedroom, and I was determined to see which. They laid me on a couch, I motioned for air, they were compelled to open the window, and you had your chance."

"How did that help you?"

"It was all-important. When a woman thinks that her house is on fire, her instinct is at once to rush to the thing which she values most. It is a perfectly overpowering impulse, and I have more than once taken advantage of it. In the case of the Darlington substitution scandal it was of use to me, and also in the Arnsworth Castle business. A married woman grabs at her baby; an unmarried one reaches for her jewel-box. Now it was clear to me that our lady of today had nothing in the house more precious to her than what we are in quest of. She would rush to secure it. The alarm of fire was admirably done. The smoke and shouting were enough to shake nerves of steel. She responded beautifully. The photograph is in a recess behind a sliding panel just above the right bell-pull. She was there in an instant, and I caught a glimpse of it as she half-drew it out. When I cried out that it was a false alarm, she replaced it, glanced at the rocket, rushed from the room, and I have not seen her since. I rose, and, making my excuses, escaped from the house. I hesitated whether to attempt to secure the photograph at once; but the coachman had come in, and as he was watching me narrowly it seemed safer to wait. A little over-precipitance may ruin all."

"And now?" I asked.

"Our quest is practically finished. I shall call with the King tomorrow, and with you, if you care to come with us. We will be shown into the sitting-room to wait for the lady, but it is probable that when she comes she may find neither us nor the photograph. It might be a satisfaction to his Majesty to regain it with his own hands."

"And when will you call?"

"At eight in the morning. She will not be up, so that we shall have a clear field. Besides, we must be prompt, for this marriage may mean a complete change in her life and habits. I must wire to the King without delay."

We had reached Baker Street and had stopped at the door. He was searching his pockets for the key when someone passing said:

"Good-night, Mister Sherlock Holmes."

There were several people on the pavement at the time, but the greeting appeared to come from a slim youth in an ulster who had hurried by.

"I've heard that voice before," said Holmes, staring down the dimly lit street. "Now, I wonder who the deuce that could have been."

3

I slept at Baker Street that night, and we were engaged upon our toast and coffee in the morning when the King of Bohemia rushed into the room.

"You have really got it!" he cried, grasping Sherlock Holmes by either shoulder and looking eagerly into his face.

"Not yet."

"But you have hopes?"

"I have hopes."

"Then, come. I am all impatience to be gone."

"We must have a cab."

"No, my brougham is waiting."

"Then that will simplify matters." We descended and started off once more for Briony Lodge.

"Irene Adler is married," remarked Holmes.

"Married! When?"

"Yesterday."

"But to whom?"

"To an English lawyer named Norton."

"But she could not love him."

"I am in hopes that she does."

"And why in hopes?"

"Because it would spare your Majesty all fear of future annoyance. If the lady loves her husband, she does not love your Majesty. If she does not love your Majesty, there is no reason why she should interfere with your Majesty's plan."

"It is true. And yet—Well! I wish she had been of my own station! What a queen she would have made!" He relapsed into a moody silence, which was not broken until we drew up in Serpentine Avenue.

The door of Briony Lodge was open, and an elderly woman stood upon the steps. She watched us with a sardonic eye as we stepped from the brougham.

"Mr. Sherlock Holmes, I believe?" said she.

"I am Mr. Holmes," answered my companion, looking at her with a questioning and rather startled gaze.

"Indeed! My mistress told me that you were likely to call. She left this morning with her husband by the 5.15 train from Charing Cross for the Continent."

"What!" Sherlock Holmes staggered back, white with chagrin and surprise. "Do you mean that she has left England?"

"Never to return."

"And the papers?" asked the King hoarsely. "All is lost."

"We shall see," he pushed past the servant and rushed into the drawing-room, followed by the King and myself. The furniture was scattered about in every direction, with dismantled shelves and open drawers, as if the lady had hurriedly ransacked them before her flight. Holmes rushed at the bell-pull, tore back a small sliding shutter, and, plunging in his hand, pulled out a photograph and a letter. The photograph was of Irene Adler herself in evening dress, the letter was superscribed to "Sherlock Holmes, Esq. To be left till called for." My friend tore it open and we all three read it together. It was dated at midnight of the preceding night and ran in this way:

"My dear Mr. Sherlock Holmes:

"You really did it very well. You took me in completely. Until after the alarm of fire, I had not a suspicion. But then, when I found how I had betrayed myself, I began to think. I had been warned against you months ago. I had been told that if the King employed an agent it would certainly be you. And your address had been given me. Yet, with all this, you made me reveal what you wanted to know. Even after I became suspicious, I found it hard to think evil of such a dear, kind old clergyman. But, you know, I have been trained as an actress myself. Male costume is nothing new to me. I often take advantage of the freedom which it gives. I sent John, the coachman, to watch you, ran up stairs, got into my walking-clothes, as I call them, and came down just as you departed.

"Well, I followed you to your door, and so made sure that I was really an object of interest to the celebrated Mr. Sherlock Holmes. Then I, rather imprudently, wished you good-night, and started for the Temple to see my husband.

"We both thought the best resource was flight, when pursued by so formidable an antagonist; so you will find the nest empty when you call tomorrow. As to the photograph, your client may rest in peace. I love and am loved by a better man than he. The King may do what he will without hindrance from one whom he has cruelly wronged. I keep it only to safeguard myself, and to preserve a weapon which will always secure me from any steps which he might take in the future. I leave a photograph which he might care to possess; and I remain, dear Mr. Sherlock Holmes.

"Very truly yours,
"Irene Norton, née Adler."

"What a woman—oh, what a woman!" cried the King of Bohemia, when we had all three read this epistle. "Did I not tell you how quick and resolute she was? Would she not have made an admirable queen? Is it not a pity that she was not on my level?"

"From what I have seen of the lady she seems indeed to be on a very different level to your Majesty," said Holmes coldly. "I am sorry that I have not been able to bring your Majesty's business to a more successful conclusion."

"On the contrary, my dear sir," cried the King; "nothing could be more successful. I know that her word is inviolate. The photograph is now as safe as if it were in the fire."

"I am glad to hear your Majesty say so."

"I am immensely indebted to you. Pray tell me in what way I can reward you. This ring—" He slipped an emerald snake ring from his finger and held it out upon the palm of his hand.

"Your Majesty has something which I should value even more highly," said Holmes.

"You have but to name it."

"This photograph!"

The King stared at him in amazement.

"Irene's photograph!" he cried. "Certainly, if you wish it."

"I thank your Majesty. Then there is no more to be done in the matter. I have the honour to wish you a very good-morning." He bowed, and, turning away without observing the hand which the King had stretched out to him, he set off in my company for his chambers.

And that was how a great scandal threatened to affect the kingdom of Bohemia, and how the best plans of Mr. Sherlock Holmes were beaten by a woman's wit. He used to make merry over the cleverness of women, but I have not heard him do it of late. And when he speaks of Irene Adler, or when he refers to her photograph, it is always under the honourable title of the woman.

STORY 3

NOBODY'S STORY

Charles Dickens

He lived on the bank of a mighty river, broad and deep, which was always silently rolling on to a vast undiscovered ocean. It had rolled on, ever since the world began. It had changed its course sometimes, and turned into new channels, leaving its old ways dry and barren; but it had ever been upon the flow, and ever was to flow until Time should be no more. Against its strong, unfathomable stream, nothing made head. No living creature, no flower, no leaf, no particle of animate or inanimate existence, ever strayed back from the undiscovered ocean. The tide of the river set resistlessly towards it; and the tide never stopped, any more than the earth stops in its circling round the sun.

He lived in a busy place, and he worked very hard to live. He had no hope of ever being rich enough to live a month without hard work, but he was quite content, GOD knows, to labour with a cheerful will. He was one of an immense family, all of whose sons and daughters gained their daily bread by daily work, prolonged from their rising up betimes until their lying down at night. Beyond this destiny he had no prospect, and he sought none.

There was over-much drumming, trumpeting, and speech-making, in the neighbourhood where he dwelt; but he had nothing to do with that. Such clash and uproar came from the Bigwig family, at the unaccountable proceedings of which race, he marvelled much. They set up the strangest statues, in iron, marble, bronze, and brass, before his door; and darkened his house with the legs and tails of uncouth images of horses. He wondered what it all meant, smiled in a rough good-humoured way he had, and kept at his hard work.

The Bigwig family (composed of all the stateliest people thereabouts, and all the noisiest) had undertaken to save him the trouble of thinking for himself, and to manage him and his affairs. "Why truly," said he, "I have little time upon my hands; and if you will be so good as to take care of me, in return for the money I pay over"—for the Bigwig family were not above his money—"I shall be relieved and much obliged, considering that you know best." Hence the drumming, trumpeting, and speech-making, and the ugly images of horses which he was expected to fall down and worship.

"I don't understand all this," said he, rubbing his furrowed brow confusedly. "But it HAS a meaning, maybe, if I could find it out."

"It means," returned the Bigwig family, suspecting something of what he said, "honour and glory in the highest, to the highest merit."

"Oh!" said he. And he was glad to hear that.

But, when he looked among the images in iron, marble, bronze, and brass, he failed to find a rather meritorious countryman of his, once the son of a Warwickshire wool-dealer, or any single countryman whomsoever of that kind. He could find none of the men whose knowledge had rescued him and his children from terrific and disfiguring disease, whose boldness had raised his forefathers from the condition of serfs, whose wise fancy had opened a new and high existence to the humblest, whose skill had filled the working man's world with accumulated wonders. Whereas, he did find others whom he knew no good of, and even others whom he knew much ill of.

"Humph!" said he. "I don't quite understand it."

So, he went home, and sat down by his fireside to get it out of his mind.

Now, his fireside was a bare one, all hemmed in by blackened streets; but it was a precious place to him. The hands of his wife were hardened with toil, and she was old before her time; but she was dear to him. His children, stunted in their growth, bore traces of unwholesome nurture; but they had beauty in his sight. Above all other things, it was an earnest desire of this man's soul that his children should be taught. "If I am sometimes misled," said he, "for want of knowledge, at least let them know better, and avoid my mistakes. If it is hard to me to reap the harvest of pleasure and instruction that is stored in books, let it be easier to them."

But, the Bigwig family broke out into violent family quarrels concerning what it was lawful to teach to this man's children. Some of the family insisted on such a thing being primary and indispensable above all other things; and others of the family insisted on such another thing being primary and indispensable above all other things; and the Bigwig family, rent into factions, wrote pamphlets, held convocations, delivered charges, orations, and all varieties of discourses; impounded one another in courts Lay and courts Ecclesiastical; threw dirt, exchanged pummelings, and fell together by the ears in unintelligible animosity. Meanwhile, this man, in his short evening snatches at his fireside, saw the demon Ignorance arise there, and take his children to itself. He saw his daughter perverted into a heavy, slatternly drudge; he saw his son go moping down the ways of low sensuality, to brutality and crime; he saw the dawning light of intelligence in the eyes of his babies so changing into cunning and suspicion, that he could have rather wished them idiots.

"I don't understand this any the better," said he; "but I think it cannot be right. Nay, by the clouded Heaven above me, I protest against this as my wrong!"

Becoming peaceable again (for his passion was usually short-lived, and his nature kind), he looked about him on his Sundays and holidays, and he saw how much monotony and weariness there was, and thence how drunkenness arose with all its train of ruin. Then he appealed to the Bigwig family, and said, "We are a labouring people, and I have a glimmering suspicion in me that labouring people of whatever condition were made—by a higher intelligence than yours, as I poorly understand it—to be in need of mental refreshment and recreation. See what we fall into, when we rest without it. Come! Amuse me harmlessly, show me something, give me an escape!"

But, here the Bigwig family fell into a state of uproar absolutely deafening. When some few voices were faintly heard, proposing to show him the wonders of the world, the greatness of creation, the mighty changes of time, the workings of nature and the beauties of art—to show him these things, that is to say, at any period of his life when he could look upon them—there arose among the Bigwigs such roaring and raving, such pulpiting and petitioning, such maundering and memorialising, such name-calling and dirt-throwing, such a shrill wind of parliamentary questioning and feeble replying—where "I dare not" waited on "I would"—that the poor fellow stood aghast, staring wildly around.

"Have I provoked all this," said he, with his hands to his affrighted ears, "by what was meant to be an innocent request, plainly arising out of my familiar experience, and the common knowledge of all men who choose to open their eyes? I don't understand, and I am not understood. What is to come of such a state of things!"

He was bending over his work, often asking himself the question, when the news began to spread that a pestilence had appeared among the labourers, and was slaying them by thousands. Going forth to look about him, he soon found this to be true. The dying and the dead were mingled in the close and tainted houses among which his life was passed. New poison was distilled into the always murky, always sickening air. The robust and the weak, old age and infancy, the father and the mother, all were stricken down alike.

What means of flight had he? He remained there, where he was, and saw those who were dearest to him die. A kind preacher came to him, and would have said some prayers to soften his heart in his gloom, but he replied:

"O what avails it, missionary, to come to me, a man condemned to residence in this foetid place, where every sense bestowed upon me for my delight becomes a torment, and where every minute of my numbered days is new mire added to the heap under which I lie oppressed! But, give me my first glimpse of Heaven, through a little of its light and air; give me pure water; help me to be clean; lighten this heavy atmosphere and heavy life, in which our spirits sink, and we become the indifferent and callous creatures you too often see us; gently and kindly take the bodies of those who die among us, out of the small room where we grow to be so familiar with the awful change that even its sanctity is lost to us; and, Teacher, then I will hear—none know better than you, how willingly—of Him whose thoughts were so much with the poor, and who had compassion for all human sorrow!"

He was at work again, solitary and sad, when his Master came and stood near to him dressed in black. He, also, had suffered heavily. His young wife, his beautiful and good young wife, was dead; so, too, his only child.

"Master, 'tis hard to bear—I know it—but be comforted. I would give you comfort, if I could."

The Master thanked him from his heart, but, said he, "O you labouring men! The calamity began among you. If you had but lived more healthily and decently, I should not be the widowed and bereft mourner that I am this day."

"Master," returned the other, shaking his head, "I have begun to understand a little that most calamities will come from us, as this one did, and that none will stop at our poor doors, until we are united with that great squabbling family yonder, to do the things that are right. We cannot live healthily and decently, unless they who undertook to manage us provide the means. We cannot be instructed unless they will teach us; we cannot be rationally amused, unless they will amuse us; we cannot but have some false gods of our own, while they set up so many of theirs in all the public places. The evil consequences of imperfect instruction, the evil consequences of pernicious neglect, the evil consequences of unnatural restraint and the denial of humanising enjoyments, will all come from us, and none of them will stop with us. They will spread far and wide. They always do; they always have done—just like the pestilence. I understand so much, I think, at last."

But the Master said again, "O you labouring men! How seldom do we ever hear of you, except in connection with some trouble!"

"Master," he replied, "I am Nobody, and little likely to be heard of (nor yet much wanted to be heard of, perhaps), except when there is some trouble. But it never begins with me, and it never can end with me. As sure as Death, it comes down to me, and it goes up from me."

There was so much reason in what he said, that the Bigwig family, getting wind of it, and being horribly frightened by the late desolation, resolved to unite with him to do the things that were right—at all events, so far as the said things were associated with the direct prevention, humanly speaking, of another pestilence. But, as their fear wore off, which it soon began to do, they resumed their falling out among themselves, and did nothing. Consequently the scourge appeared again—low down as before—and spread avengingly upward as before, and carried off vast numbers of the brawlers. But not a man among them ever admitted, if in the least degree he ever perceived, that he had anything to do with it.

So Nobody lived and died in the old, old, old way; and this, in the main, is the whole of Nobody's story.

Had he no name, you ask? Perhaps it was Legion. It matters little what his name was. Let us call him Legion.

If you were ever in the Belgian villages near the field of Waterloo, you will have seen, in some quiet little church, a monument erected by faithful companions in arms to the memory of Colonel A, Major B, Captains C, D and E, Lieutenants F and G, Ensigns H, I and J, seven non-commissioned officers, and one hundred and thirty rank and file, who fell in the discharge of their duty on the memorable day. The story of Nobody is the story of the rank and file of the earth. They bear their share of the battle; they have their part in the victory; they fall; they leave no name but in the mass. The march of the proudest of us, leads to the dusty way by which they go. O! Let us think of them this year at the Christmas fire, and not forget them when it is burnt out.

STORY 4

ARABY

James Joyce

North Richmond Street, being blind, was a quiet street except at the hour when the Christian Brothers' School set the boy free. An uninhabited house of two stories stood at the blind end, detached from its neighbours in a square ground. The other houses of the street, conscious of decent lives within them, gazed at one another with brown imperturbable faces.

The former tenant of our house, a priest, had died in the back drawing-room. Air, musty from having been long enclosed, hung in all the rooms, and the waste room behind the kitchen was littered with old useless papers. Among these I found a few paper-covered books, the pages of which were curled and damp: *The Abbot,* by Walter Scott, *The Devout Communicant* and *The Memoirs of Vidocq.* I liked the last best because its leaves were yellow. The wild garden behind the house contained a central apple-tree and a few straggling bushes, under one of which I found the late tenant's rusty bicycle-pump. He had been a very charitable priest; in his will he had left all his money to institutions and the furniture of his house to his sister.

When the short days of winter came, dusk fell before we had well eaten our dinners. When we met in the street the houses had grown sombre. The space of sky above us was the colour of ever-changing violet and towards it the lamps of the street lifted their feeble lanterns. The cold air stung us and we played till our bodies glowed. Our shouts echoed in the silent street. The career of our play brought us through the dark muddy lanes behind the houses, where we ran the gauntlet of the rough tribes from the cottages, to the back doors of the dark dripping gardens where odours arose from the ashpits, to the dark odorous stables where a coachman smoothed and combed the horse or shook music from the buckled harness. When we returned, the street light from the kitchen windows had filled the areas. If my uncle was seen turning the corner, we hid in the shadow until we had seen him safely housed. Of if Mangan's sister came out on the doorstep to call her brother in to his tea, we watched her from our shadow peer up and down the street. We waited to see whether she would remain or go in and, if she remained, we left our shadow and walked up to Mangan's steps resignedly. She was waiting for us, her figure defined by the light from the half-opened door, Her brother always teased her before he obeyed, and I stood by the railings looking at her. Her dress swung as she moved her body, and the soft rope of her hair tossed from side to side.

Every morning I lay on the floor in the front parlour watching her door. The blind was pulled down to within an inch of the sash so that I could not be seen. When she came out on the doorstep, my heart leaped. I ran to the hall, seized my books and followed her. I kept her brown figure always in my eye and, when we came near the point at which our ways diverged, I quickened my pace and passed her. This happened morning after morning. I had never spoken to her except for a few casual words, and yet her name was like a summons to all my foolish blood.

Her image accompanied me even in places the most hostile to romance. On Saturday evenings when my aunt went marketing, I had to go to carry some of the parcels. We walked through the flaring streets, jostled by drunken men and bargaining women, amid the curses of labourers, the shrill litanies of shop-boys who stood on guard by the barrels of pigs' cheeks, the nasal chanting of street-singers, who sang a *Come-all-you* about O'Donovan Rossa, or a ballad about the troubles in our native land. These noises converged in a single sensation of life for me: I imagined that I bore my chalice safely through a throng of foes. Her name sprang to my lips at moments in strange prayers and praises which I myself did not understand. My eyes were often full of tears (I could not tell why) and at times a flood from my heart seemed to pour itself out into my bosom. I thought little of the future. I did not know whether I would ever speak to her or not or, if I spoke to her, how I could tell her of my confused adoration. But my body was like a harp and her words and gestures were like fingers running upon the wires.

One evening I went into the back drawing-room in which the priest had died. It was a dark rainy evening and there was no sound in the house. Through one of the broken panes I heard the rain impinge upon the earth, the fine incessant needles of water playing in the sodden beds. Some distant lamp or lighted window gleamed blow me. I was thankful that I could see so little. All my senses seemed to desire to veil themselves and, feeling that I was about to slip from them, I pressed the palms of my hands together until they trembled, murmuring: *'O love! O love'* many times.

At last she spoke to me. When she addressed the first words to me I was so confused that I did not know what to answer. She asked me if was I going to *Araby.* I forgot whether I answered yes or no. It would be a splendid bazaar; she said she would love to go.

'And why can't you?'I asked.

While she spoke she turned a silver bracelet round and round her wrist. She could not go, she said because there would be a retreat that week in her convent. Her brother and two other boys were fighting for their caps, and I was alone at the railings. She held one of the spikes, bowing her head towards me. The light from the lamp opposite our door caught the white curve of her neck, lit up her hair that rested there and, falling, lit up the hand upon the railing. It fell over one side of her dress and caught the white border of a petticoat, just visible as she stood at ease.

'It's well for you,' she said.

'If I go,' I said, 'I will bring you something.'

What innumerable follies laid waste my waking and sleeping thoughts after that evening! I wished to annihilate the tedious intervening days. I chafed against the work of school. At night in my bedroom and by day in the classroom her image came between me and the page I strove to read.

The syllables of the word *Araby* were called to me through the silence in which my soul luxuriated and cast an Eastern enchantment over me. I asked for leave to go to the bazaar on Saturday night. My aunt was surprised, and hoped it was not some Freemason affair. I answered few questions in class. I watched my master's face pass from amiability to sternness; he hoped I was not beginning to idle, I could not call my wandering thoughts together. I had hardly any patience with the serious work of life which, now that it stood between me and my desire, seemed to me child's play, ugly, monotonous child's play.

On Saturday morning I reminded my uncle that I wished to go to the bazaar in the evening. He was fussing at the hall-stand, looking for the hat-brush, and answered me curtly:

'Yes, boy, I know.'

As he was in the hall I could not go into the front parlour and lie at the window. I left the house in bad humour and walked slowly towards the school. The air was pitilessly raw and already my heart misgave me.

When I came home to dinner my uncle had not yet been home. Still it was early. I sat staring at the clock for some time and, when its ticking began to irritate me, I left the room. I mounted the staircase and gained the upper part of the house. The high, cold, empty, gloomy rooms liberated me and I went from room to room singing. From the front window I saw my companions playing below in the street. Their cries reached me, weakened and indistinct and, leaning my forehead against the cool glass, I looked over at the dark house where she lived. I may have stood there for an hour, seeing nothing but the brown-clad figure cast by my imagination, touched discreetly by the lamplight at the curved neck, at the hand upon the railings and at the border below the dress.

When I came downstairs again I found Mrs Mercer sitting at the fire. She was an old, garrulous woman, a pawn-broker's widow, who collected used stamps for some pious purpose. I had to endure the gossip of the tea-table. The meal was prolonged beyond an hour and still my uncle did not come. Mrs Mercer stood upto go: she was sorry she couldn't wait any longer, but it was after eight o'clock and she did not like to be out late, as the night air was bad for her. When she had gone, I began to walk up and down the room, clenching my fists. My aunt said:

'I'm afraid you may put off your bazaar for this night of Our Lord.'

At nine o'clock I heard my uncle's latch-key in the hall door. I heard him talking to himself and heard the hallstand rocking when it had received the weight of his overcoat. I could interpret these signs. When he was midway through his dinner, I asked him to give me the money to go to the bazaar. He had forgotten.

'The people are in bed and after their first sleep now,' he said.

I did not smile. My aunt said to him energetically:

'Can't you give him the money and let him go? You've kept him late enough as it is.'

My uncle said he was very sorry he had forgotten. He said he believed in the old saying: 'All work and no play makes Jack a dull boy.' He asked me where I was going and, when I had told him a second time, he asked me did I know *The Arab's*

Farewell to his Steed. When I left the kitchen, he was about to recite the opening lines of the piece to my aunt.

I held a florin tightly in my hand as I strode down Buckingham Street towards the station. The sight of the streets thronged with buyers and glaring with gas recalled to me the purpose of my journey. I took my seat in a third-class carriage of a deserted train. After an intolerable delay the train moved out of the station slowly. It crept onward among ruinous houses and over the twinkling river. At Westland Row Station a crowd of people pressed to the carriage doors, but the porters moved them back, saying that it was special train for the bazaar. I remained alone in the bare carriage. In a few minutes the train drew up beside an improvised wooden platform. I passed out on to the road and saw by the lighted dial of a clock that it was ten minutes to ten. In front of me was a large building which displayed the magical name.

I could not find any sixpenny entrance and, fearing that the bazaar would be closed, I passed in quickly through a turnstile, handing a shilling to a weary-looking man. I found myself in a big hall girded at half its height by a gallery. Nearly all the stalls were closed and the greater part of the hall was in darkness. I recognised a silence like that which pervades a church after a service. I walked into the centre of the bazaar timidly. A few people were gathered about the stalls which were still open. Before a curtain, over which the words *Cafe Chantant* were written in coloured lamps, two men were counting money on a salver. I listened to the fall of the coins.

Remembering with difficulty why I had come, I went over to one of the stalls and examined porcelain vases and flowered tea-sets. At the door of the stall a young lady was talking and laughing with two young gentlemen. I marked their English accents and listened vaguely to their conversation

'O, I never said such a thing!'

'O, but you did!'

'O, but I didn't!'

'Didn't she say that?'

'Yes. I heard her.'

'O, there's a...fib!'

Observing me, the young lady came over and asked me did I wish to buy anything. The tone of her voice was not encouraging; she seemed to have spoken to me out of a sense of duty. I looked humbly at the great jars that stood like eastern guards at either side of the dark entrance to the stall and murmured:

'No, thank you.'

The young lady changed the position of one of the vases and went back to the two young men. They began to talk of the same subject. Once or twice the young lady glanced at me over her shoulder.

I lingered before her stall, though I knew my stay was useless, to make my interest in her wares seem the more real. Then I turned away slowly and walked down the middle of the bazaar. I allowed the two pennies to fall against the sixpence in my pocket. I heard a voice call from one end of the gallery that the light was out. The upper part of the hall was now completely dark.

Gazing up into the darkness I saw myself as a creature driven and derided by vanity; and my eyes burned with anguish and anger.

STORY 5

A MODEST PROPOSAL

Jonathan Swift

It is a melancholy object to those, who walk through this great town, or travel in the country, when they see the streets, the roads and cabbin-doors crowded with beggars of the female sex, followed by three, four, or six children, all in rags, and importuning every passenger for an alms. These mothers instead of being able to work for their honest livelihood, are forced to employ all their time in stroling to beg sustenance for their helpless infants who, as they grow up, either turn thieves for want of work, or leave their dear native country, to fight for the Pretender in Spain, or sell themselves to the Barbadoes.

I think it is agreed by all parties, that this prodigious number of children in the arms, or on the backs, or at the heels of their mothers, and frequently of their fathers, is in the present deplorable state of the kingdom, a very great additional grievance; and therefore whoever could find out a fair, cheap and easy method of making these children sound and useful members of the common-wealth, would deserve so well of the publick, as to have his statue set up for a preserver of the nation.

But my intention is very far from being confined to provide only for the children of professed beggars: it is of a much greater extent, and shall take in the whole number of infants at a certain age, who are born of parents in effect as little able to support them, as those who demand our charity in the streets.

As to my own part, having turned my thoughts for many years, upon this important subject, and maturely weighed the several schemes of our projectors, I have always found them grossly mistaken in their computation. It is true, a child just dropped from its dam, may be supported by her milk, for a solar year, with little other nourishment: at most not above the value of two shillings, which the mother may certainly get, or the value in scraps, by her lawful occupation of begging; and it is exactly at one year old that I propose to provide for them in such a manner, as, instead of being a charge upon their parents, or the parish, or wanting food and raiment for the rest of their lives, they shall, on the contrary, contribute to the feeding, and partly to the cloathing of many thousands.

There is likewise another great advantage in my scheme, that it will prevent those voluntary abortions, and that horrid practice of women murdering their bastard children, alas! too frequent among us, sacrificing the poor innocent babes, I doubt, more to avoid the expense than the shame, which would move tears and pity in the most savage and inhuman breast.

The number of souls in this kingdom being usually reckoned one million and a half, of these I calculate there may be about two hundred thousand couple whose wives are breeders; from which number I subtract thirty thousand couple, who are able to maintain their own children, (although I apprehend there cannot be so many, under the present distresses of the kingdom) but this being granted, there will remain an hundred and seventy thousand breeders. I again subtract fifty thousand, for those women who miscarry, or whose children die by accident or disease within the year. There only remain an hundred and twenty thousand children of poor parents annually born. The question therefore is, how this number shall be reared, and provided for? which, as I have already said, under the present situation of affairs, is utterly impossible by all the methods hitherto proposed. For we can neither employ them in handicraft or agriculture; we neither build houses, (I mean in the country) nor cultivate land: they can very seldom pick up a livelihood by stealing till they arrive at six years old; except where they are of towardly parts, although I confess they learn the rudiments much earlier; during which time they can however be properly looked upon only as probationers: As I have been informed by a principal gentleman in the county of Cavan, who protested to me, that he never knew above one or two instances under the age of six, even in a part of the kingdom so renowned for the quickest proficiency in that art.

I am assured by our merchants, that a boy or a girl before twelve years old, is no saleable commodity, and even when they come to this age, they will not yield above three pounds, or three pounds and half a crown at most, on the exchange; which cannot turn to account either to the parents or kingdom, the charge of nutriments and rags having been at least four times that value.

I shall now therefore humbly propose my own thoughts, which I hope will not be liable to the least objection.

I have been assured by a very knowing American of my acquaintance in London, that a young healthy child well nursed, is, at a year old, a most delicious nourishing and wholesome food, whether stewed, roasted, baked, or boiled; and I make no doubt that it will equally serve in a fricasie, or a ragoust.

I do therefore humbly offer it to publick consideration, that of the hundred and twenty thousand children, already computed, twenty thousand may be reserved for breed, whereof only one fourth part to be males; which is more than we allow to sheep, black cattle, or swine, and my reason is, that these children are seldom the fruits of marriage, a circumstance not much regarded by our savages, therefore, one male will be sufficient to serve four females. That the remaining hundred thousand may, at a year old, be offered in sale to the persons of quality and fortune, through the kingdom, always advising the mother to let them suck plentifully in the last month, so as to render them plump, and fat for a good table. A child will make two dishes at an entertainment for friends, and when the family dines alone, the fore or hind quarter will make a reasonable dish, and seasoned with a little pepper or salt, will be very good boiled on the fourth day, especially in winter.

I have reckoned upon a medium, that a child just born will weigh 12 pounds, and in a solar year, if tolerably nursed, encreaseth to 28 pounds.

I grant this food will be somewhat dear, and therefore very proper for landlords, who, as they have already devoured most of the parents, seem to have the best title to the children.

Infant's flesh will be in season throughout the year, but more plentiful in March, and a little before and after; for we are told by a grave author, an eminent French physician, that fish being a prolifick dyet, there are more children born in Roman Catholick countries about nine months after Lent, the markets will be more glutted than usual, because the number of Popish infants, is at least three to one in this kingdom, and therefore it will have one other collateral advantage, by lessening the number of Papists among us.

I have already computed the charge of nursing a beggar's child (in which list I reckon all cottagers, labourers, and four-fifths of the farmers) to be about two shillings per annum, rags included; and I believe no gentleman would repine to give ten shillings for the carcass of a good fat child, which, as I have said, will make four dishes of excellent nutritive meat, when he hath only some particular friend, or his own family to dine with him. Thus the squire will learn to be a good landlord, and grow popular among his tenants, the mother will have eight shillings neat profit, and be fit for work till she produces another child.

Those who are more thrifty (as I must confess the times require) may flea the carcass; the skin of which, artificially dressed, will make admirable gloves for ladies, and summer boots for fine gentlemen.

As to our City of Dublin, shambles may be appointed for this purpose, in the most convenient parts of it, and butchers we may be assured will not be wanting; although I rather recommend buying the children alive, and dressing them hot from the knife, as we do roasting pigs.

A very worthy person, a true lover of his country, and whose virtues I highly esteem, was lately pleased, in discoursing on this matter, to offer a refinement upon my scheme. He said, that many gentlemen of this kingdom, having of late destroyed their deer, he conceived that they want of venison might be well supply'd by the bodies of young lads and maidens, not exceeding fourteen years of age, nor under twelve; so great a number of both sexes in every country being now ready to starve for want of work and service: And these to be disposed of by their parents if alive, or otherwise by their nearest relations. But with due deference to so excellent a friend, and so deserving a patriot, I cannot be altogether in his sentiments; for as to the males, my American acquaintance assured me from frequent experience, that their flesh was generally tough and lean, like that of our school-boys, by continual exercise, and their taste disagreeable, and to fatten them would not answer the charge. Then as to the females, it would, I think, with humble submission, be a loss to the publick, because they soon would become breeders themselves: And besides, it is not improbable that some scrupulous people might be apt to censure such a practice, (although indeed very unjustly) as a little bordering upon cruelty, which, I confess, hath always been with me the strongest objection against any project, how well so ever intended.

But in order to justify my friend, he confessed, that this expedient was put into his head by the famous Salmanaazor, a native of the island Formosa, who came from thence to London, above twenty years ago, and in conversation told my friend, that in his country, when any young person happened to be put to death, the executioner sold the carcass to persons of quality, as a prime dainty; and that, in his time, the body of a plump girl of fifteen, who was crucified for an attempt to poison the Emperor, was sold to his imperial majesty's prime minister of state, and other great mandarins of the court in joints from the gibbet, at four hundred crowns. Neither indeed can I deny, that if the same use were made of several plump young girls in this town, who without one single groat to their fortunes, cannot stir abroad without a chair, and appear at a play-house and assemblies in foreign fineries which they never will pay for; the kingdom would not be the worse.

Some persons of a desponding spirit are in great concern about that vast number of poor people, who are aged, diseased, or maimed; and I have been desired to employ my thoughts what course may be taken, to ease the nation of so grievous an incumbrance. But I am not in the least pain upon that matter, because it is very well known, that they are every day dying, and rotting, by cold and famine, and filth, and vermin, as fast as can be reasonably expected. And as to the young labourers, they are now in almost as hopeful a condition. They cannot get work, and consequently pine away from want of nourishment, to a degree, that if at any time they are accidentally hired to common labour, they have not strength to perform it, and thus the country and themselves are happily delivered from the evils to come.

I have too long digressed, and therefore shall return to my subject. I think the advantages by the proposal which I have made are obvious and many, as well as of the highest importance.

For first, as I have already observed, it would greatly lessen the number of Papists, with whom we are yearly over-run, being the principal breeders of the nation, as well as our most dangerous enemies, and who stay at home on purpose with a design to deliver the kingdom to the Pretender, hoping to take their advantage by the absence of so many good Protestants, who have chosen rather to leave their country, than stay at home and pay tithes against their conscience to an episcopal curate.

Secondly, The poorer tenants will have something valuable of their own, which by law may be made liable to a distress, and help to pay their landlord's rent, their corn and cattle being already seized, and money a thing unknown.

Thirdly, Whereas the maintenance of an hundred thousand children, from two years old, and upwards, cannot be computed at less than ten shillings a piece per annum, the nation's stock will be thereby encreased fifty thousand pounds per annum, besides the profit of a new dish, introduced to the tables of all gentlemen of fortune in the kingdom, who have any refinement in taste. And the money will circulate among ourselves, the goods being entirely of our own growth and manufacture.

Fourthly, The constant breeders, besides the gain of eight shillings sterling per annum by the sale of their children, will be rid of the charge of maintaining them after the first year.

Fifthly, This food would likewise bring great custom to taverns, where the vintners will certainly be so prudent as to procure the best receipts for dressing it to perfection;

and consequently have their houses frequented by all the fine gentlemen, who justly value themselves upon their knowledge in good eating; and a skilful cook, who understands how to oblige his guests, will contrive to make it as expensive as they please.

Sixthly, this would be a great inducement to marriage, which all wise nations have either encouraged by rewards, or enforced by laws and penalties. It would encrease the care and tenderness of mothers towards their children, when they were sure of a settlement for life to the poor babes, provided in some sort by the publick, to their annual profit instead of expence. We should soon see an honest emulation among the married women, which of them could bring the fattest child to the market. Men would become as fond of their wives, during the time of their pregnancy, as they are now of their mares in foal, their cows in calf, or sow when they are ready to farrow; nor offer to beat or kick them (as is too frequent a practice) for fear of a miscarriage.

Many other advantages might be enumerated. For instance, the addition of some thousand carcasses in our exportation of barrel'd beef: the propagation of swine's flesh, and improvement in the art of making good bacon, so much wanted among us by the great destruction of pigs, too frequent at our tables; which are no way comparable in taste or magnificence to a well grown, fat yearly child, which roasted whole will make a considerable figure at a Lord Mayor's feast, or any other publick entertainment. But this, and many others, I omit, being studious of brevity.

Supposing that one thousand families in this city, would be constant customers for infants flesh, besides others who might have it at merry meetings, particularly at weddings and christenings, I compute that Dublin would take off annually about twenty thousand carcasses; and the rest of the kingdom (where probably they will be sold somewhat cheaper) the remaining eighty thousand.

I can think of no one objection, that will possibly be raised against this proposal, unless it should be urged, that the number of people will be thereby much lessened in the kingdom. This I freely own, and 'twas indeed one principal design in offering it to the world. I desire the reader will observe, that I calculate my remedy for this one individual Kingdom of Ireland, and for no other that ever was, is, or, I think, ever can be upon Earth. Therefore let no man talk to me of other expedients: Of taxing our absentees at five shillings a pound: Of using neither cloaths, nor household furniture, except what is of our own growth and manufacture: Of utterly rejecting the materials and instruments that promote foreign luxury: Of curing the expensiveness of pride, vanity, idleness, and gaming in our women: Of introducing a vein of parsimony, prudence and temperance: Of learning to love our country, wherein we differ even from Laplanders, and the inhabitants of Topinamboo: Of quitting our animosities and factions, nor acting any longer like the Jews, who were murdering one another at the very moment their city was taken: Of being a little cautious not to sell our country and consciences for nothing: Of teaching landlords to have at least one degree of mercy towards their tenants. Lastly, of putting a spirit of honesty, industry, and skill into our shop-keepers, who, if a resolution could now be taken to buy only our native goods, would immediately unite to cheat and exact upon us in the price, the measure, and the goodness, nor could ever yet be brought to make one fair proposal of just dealing, though often and earnestly invited to it.

Therefore I repeat, let no man talk to me of these and the like expedients, 'till he hath at least some glympse of hope, that there will ever be some hearty and sincere attempt to put them into practice.

But, as to myself, having been wearied out for many years with offering vain, idle, visionary thoughts, and at length utterly despairing of success, I fortunately fell upon this proposal, which, as it is wholly new, so it hath something solid and real, of no expence and little trouble, full in our own power, and whereby we can incur no danger in disobliging England. For this kind of commodity will not bear exportation, and flesh being of too tender a consistence, to admit a long continuance in salt, although perhaps I could name a country, which would be glad to eat up our whole nation without it.

After all, I am not so violently bent upon my own opinion, as to reject any offer, proposed by wise men, which shall be found equally innocent, cheap, easy, and effectual. But before something of that kind shall be advanced in contradiction to my scheme, and offering a better, I desire the author or authors will be pleased maturely to consider two points. First, as things now stand, how they will be able to find food and raiment for a hundred thousand useless mouths and backs. And secondly, There being a round million of creatures in humane figure throughout this kingdom, whose whole subsistence put into a common stock, would leave them in debt two million of pounds sterling, adding those who are beggars by profession, to the bulk of farmers, cottagers and labourers, with their wives and children, who are beggars in effect; I desire those politicians who dislike my overture, and may perhaps be so bold to attempt an answer, that they will first ask the parents of these mortals, whether they would not at this day think it a great happiness to have been sold for food at a year old, in the manner I prescribe, and thereby have avoided such a perpetual scene of misfortunes, as they have since gone through, by the oppression of landlords, the impossibility of paying rent without money or trade, the want of common sustenance, with neither house nor cloaths to cover them from the in clemencies of the weather, and the most inevitable prospect of intailing the like, or greater miseries, upon their breed forever.

I profess, in the sincerity of my heart, that I have not the least personal interest in endeavouring to promote this necessary work, having no other motive than the publick good of my country, by advancing our trade, providing for infants, relieving the poor, and giving some pleasure to the rich. I have no children, by which I can propose to get a single penny; the youngest being nine years old, and my wife past child-bearing.

STORY 6

GOD SEES THE TRUTH, BUT WAITS

Leo Tolstoy

In the town of Vladímir lived a young merchant named Iván Dmítritch Aksyónof. He had two shops and a house of his own.

Aksyónof was a handsome, fair-haired, curly-headed fellow, full of fun, and very fond of singing. When quite a young man he had been given to drink, and was riotous when he had had too much; but after he married he gave up drinking, except now and then.

One summer Aksyónof was going to the Nízhny Fair, and as he bade good-bye to his family his wife said to him, 'Iván Dmítritch, do not start to-day; I have had a bad dream about you.'

Aksyónof laughed, and said, 'You are afraid that when I get to the fair I shall go on the spree.'

His wife replied: 'I do not know what I am afraid of; all I know is that I had a bad dream. I dreamt you returned from the town, and when you took off your cap I saw that your hair was quite grey.'

Aksyónof laughed. 'That's a lucky sign,' said he. 'See if I don't sell out all my goods, and bring you some presents from the fair.'

So he said good-bye to his family, and drove away.

When he had travelled half-way, he met a merchant whom he knew, and they put up at the same inn for the night. They had some tea together, and then went to bed in adjoining rooms.

It was not Aksyónof's habit to sleep late, and, wishing to travel while it was still cool, he aroused his driver before dawn, and told him to put in the horses.

Then he made his way across to the landlord of the inn (who lived in a cottage at the back), paid his bill, and continued his journey.

When he had gone about twenty-five miles, he stopped for the horses to be fed. Aksyónof rested awhile in the passage of the inn, then he stepped out into the porch, and, ordering a *samovár*[1] to be heated, got out his guitar and began to play.

Suddenly a *tróyka*[2] drove up with tinkling bells, and an official alighted, followed by two soldiers. He came to Aksyónof and began to question him, asking him who he was and whence he came. Aksyónof answered him fully, and said, 'Won't you have some tea with me?' But the official went on

1. The samovár ('self-boiler') is an urn in which water can be heated and kept on the boil.
2. A three-horse conveyance.

cross-questioning him and asking him, 'Where did you spend last night? Were you alone, or with a fellow-merchant? Did you see the other merchant this morning? Why did you leave the inn before dawn?'

Aksyónof wondered why he was asked all these questions, but he described all that had happened, and then added, 'Why do you cross-question me as if I were a thief or a robber? I am travelling on business of my own, and there is no need to question me.'

Then the official, calling the soldiers, said, 'I am the police-officer of this district, and I question you because the merchant with whom you spent last night has been found with his throat cut. We must search your things.'

They entered the house. The soldiers and the police-officer unstrapped Aksyónof's luggage and searched it. Suddenly the officer drew a knife out of a bag, crying, 'Whose knife is this?'

Aksyónof looked, and seeing a blood-stained knife taken from his bag, he was frightened.

'How is it there is blood on this knife?'

Aksyónof tried to answer, but could hardly utter a word, and only stammered: 'I—I don't know—not mine.'

Then the police-officer said, 'This morning the merchant was found in bed with his throat cut. You are the only person who could have done it. The house was locked from inside, and no one else was there. Here is this bloodstained knife in your bag, and your face and manner betray you! Tell me how you killed him, and how much money you stole?'

Aksyónof swore he had not done it; that he had not seen the merchant after they had had tea together; that he had no money except eight thousand roubles[3] of his own, and that the knife was not his. But his voice was broken, his face pale, and he trembled with fear as though he were guilty.

The police-officer ordered the soldiers to bind Aksyónof and to put him in the cart. As they tied his feet together and flung him into the cart, Aksyónof crossed himself and wept. His money and goods were taken from him, and he was sent to the nearest town and imprisoned there. Enquiries as to his character were made in Vladímir. The merchants and other inhabitants of that town said that in former days he used to drink and waste his time, but that he was a good man. Then the trial came on: he was charged with murdering a merchant from Ryazán, and robbing him of twenty thousand roubles.

His wife was in despair, and did not know what to believe. Her children were all quite small; one was a baby at her breast. Taking them all with her, she went to the town where her husband was in gaol. At first she was not allowed to see him; but, after much begging, she obtained permission from the officials, and was taken to him. When she saw her husband in prison-dress and in chains, shut up with thieves and criminals, she fell down, and did not come to her senses for a long time. Then she drew her children to her, and sat down near him. She told him of things at home, and asked about what

3. The value of the rouble has varied at different times from more than three shillings to less than two shillings. For the purposes of ready calculation it may be taken as two shillings. In reading these stories to children, the word 'florin' can be substituted for 'rouble' if preferred.

had happened to him. He told her all, and she asked, 'What can we do now?'

'We must petition the Tsar not to let an innocent man perish.'

His wife told him that she had sent a petition to the Tsar, but that it had not been accepted.

Aksyónof did not reply, but only looked downcast.

Then his wife said, 'It was not for nothing I dreamt your hair had turned grey. You remember? You should not have started that day.' And passing her fingers through his hair, she said: 'Ványa dearest, tell your wife the truth; was it not you who did it?'

'So you, too, suspect me!' said Aksyónof, and, hiding his face in his hands, he began to weep. Then a soldier came to say that the wife and children must go away; and Aksyónof said good-bye to his family for the last time.

When they were gone, Aksyónof recalled what had been said, and when he remembered that his wife also had suspected him, he said to himself, 'It seems that only God can know the truth; it is to Him alone we must appeal, and from Him alone expect mercy.'

And Aksyónof wrote no more petitions; gave up all hope, and only prayed to God.

Aksyónof was condemned to be flogged and sent to the mines. So he was flogged with a knout, and when the wounds made by the knout were healed, he was driven to Siberia with other convicts.

For twenty-six years Aksyónof lived as a convict in Siberia. His hair turned white as snow, and his beard grew long, thin, and grey. All his mirth went; he stooped; he walked slowly, spoke little, and never laughed, but he often prayed.

In prison Aksyónof learnt to make boots, and earned a little money, with which he bought *The Lives of the Saints.* He read this book when there was light enough in the prison; and on Sundays in the prison-church he read the lessons and sang in the choir; for his voice was still good.

The prison authorities liked Aksyónof for his meekness, and his fellow-prisoners respected him: they called him 'Grandfather,' and 'The Saint.' When they wanted to petition the prison authorities about anything, they always made Aksyónof their spokesman, and when there were quarrels among the prisoners they came to him to put things right, and to judge the matter.

No news reached Aksyónof from his home, and he did not even know if his wife and children were still alive.

One day a fresh gang of convicts came to the prison. In the evening the old prisoners collected round the new ones and asked them what towns or villages they came from, and what they were sentenced for. Among the rest Aksyónof sat down near the new-comers, and listened with downcast air to what was said.

One of the new convicts, a tall, strong man of sixty, with a closely-cropped grey beard, was telling the others what he had been arrested for.

'Well, friends,' he said, 'I only took a horse that was tied to a sledge, and I was arrested and accused of stealing. I said I had only taken it to get home quicker, and had then let it go; besides, the driver was a personal friend of mine. So I said,

"It's all right." "No," said they, "you stole it." But how or where I stole it they could not say. I once really did something wrong, and ought by rights to have come here long ago, but that time I was not found out. Now I have been sent here for nothing at all. . . . Eh, but it's lies I'm telling you; I've been to Siberia before, but I did not stay long.'

'Where are you from?' asked some one.

'From Vladímir. My family are of that town. My name is Makár, and they also call me Semyónitch.'

Aksyónof raised his head and said: 'Tell me, Semyónitch, do you know anything of the merchants Aksyónof, of Vladímir? Are they still alive?'

'Know them? Of course I do. The Aksyónofs are rich, though their father is in Siberia: a sinner like ourselves, it seems! As for you, Gran'dad, how did you come here?'

Aksyónof did not like to speak of his misfortune. He only sighed, and said, 'For my sins I have been in prison these twenty-six years.'

'What sins?' asked Makár Semyónitch.

But Aksyónof only said, 'Well, well—I must have deserved it!' He would have said no more, but his companions told the new-comer how Aksyónof came to be in Siberia: how someone had killed a merchant, and had put a knife among Aksyónof's things, and Aksyónof had been unjustly condemned.

When Makár Semyónitch heard this, he looked at Aksyónof, slapped his own knee, and exclaimed, 'Well, this is wonderful! Really wonderful! But how old you've grown, Gran'dad!'

The others asked him why he was so surprised, and where he had seen Aksyónof before; but Makár Semyónitch did not reply. He only said: 'It's wonderful that we should meet here, lads!'

These words made Aksyónof wonder whether this man knew who had killed the merchant; so he said, 'Perhaps, Semyónitch, you have heard of that affair, or maybe you've seen me before?'

'How could I help hearing? The world's full of rumours. But it's long ago, and I've forgotten what I heard.'

'Perhaps you heard who killed the merchant?' asked Aksyónof.

Makár Semyónitch laughed, and replied, 'It must have been him in whose bag the knife was found! If someone else hid the knife there, "He's not a thief till he's caught," as the saying is. How could anyone put a knife into your bag while it was under your head? It would surely have woke you up?'

When Aksyónof heard these words, he felt sure this was the man who had killed the merchant. He rose and went away. All that night Aksyónof lay awake. He felt terribly unhappy, and all sorts of images rose in his mind. There was the image of his wife as she was when he parted from her to go to the fair. He saw her as if she were present; her face and her eyes rose before him; he heard her speak and laugh. Then he saw his children, quite little, as they were at that time: one with a little cloak on, another at his mother's breast. And then he remembered himself as he used to be—young and merry. He remembered how he sat playing the guitar in the porch of the inn where he was arrested, and how free from care he had been. He saw, in his mind, the place where he was flogged, the executioner, and the people standing around; the chains, the convicts, all the twenty-six years of his prison life, and his premature old age. The thought of it all made him so wretched that he was ready to kill himself.

'And it's all that villain's doing!' thought Aksyónof. And his anger was so great against Makár Semyónitch that he longed for vengeance, even if he himself should perish for it. He kept repeating prayers all night, but could get no peace. During the day he did not go near Makár Semyónitch, nor even look at him.

A fortnight passed in this way. Aksyónof could not sleep at nights, and was so miserable that he did not know what to do.

One night as he was walking about the prison he noticed some earth that came rolling out from under one of the shelves on which the prisoners slept. He stopped to see what it was. Suddenly Makár Semyónitch crept out from under the shelf, and looked up at Aksyónof with frightened face. Aksyónof tried to pass without looking at him, but Makár seized his hand and told him that he had dug a hole under the wall, getting rid of the earth by putting it into his high-boots, and emptying it out every day on the road when the prisoners were driven to their work.

'Just you keep quiet, old man, and you shall get out too. If you blab they'll flog the life out of me, but I will kill you first.'

Aksyónof trembled with anger as he looked at his enemy. He drew his hand away, saying, 'I have no wish to escape, and you have no need to kill me; you killed me long ago! As to telling of you—I may do so or not, as God shall direct.'

Next day, when the convicts were led out to work, the convoy soldiers noticed that one or other of the prisoners emptied some earth out of his boots. The prison was searched, and the tunnel found. The Governor came and questioned all the prisoners to find out who had dug the hole. They all denied any knowledge of it. Those who knew, would not betray Makár Semyónitch, knowing he would be flogged almost to death. At last the Governor turned to Aksyónof, whom he knew to be a just man, and said:

'You are a truthful old man; tell me, before God, who dug the hole?'

Makár Semyónitch stood as if he were quite unconcerned, looking at the Governor and not so much as glancing at Aksyónof. Aksyónof's lips and hands trembled, and for a long time he could not utter a word. He thought, 'Why should I screen him who ruined my life? Let him pay for what I have suffered. But if I tell, they will probably flog the life out of him, and maybe I suspect him wrongly. And, after all, what good would it be to me?'

'Well, old man,' repeated the Governor, 'tell us the truth: who has been digging under the wall?'

Aksyónof glanced at Makár Semyónitch, and said, 'I cannot say, your honour. It is not God's will that I should tell! Do what you like with me; I am in your hands.'

However much the Governor tried, Aksyónof would say no more, and so the matter had to be left.

That night, when Aksyónof was lying on his bed and just beginning to doze, someone came quietly and sat down on his bed. He peered through the darkness and recognized Makár.

'What more do you want of me?' asked Aksyónof. 'Why have you come here?'

Makár Semyónitch was silent. So Aksyónof sat up and said, 'What do you want? Go away, or I will call the guard!'

Makár Semyónitch bent close over Aksyónof, and whispered, 'Iván Dmítritch, forgive me!'

'What for?' asked Aksyónof.

'It was I who killed the merchant and hid the knife among your things. I meant to kill you too, but I heard a noise outside; so I hid the knife in your bag and escaped out of the window.'

Aksyónof was silent, and did not know what to say. Makár Semyónitch slid off the bed-shelf and knelt upon the ground. 'Iván Dmítritch,' said he, 'forgive me! For the love of God, forgive me! I will confess that it was I who killed the merchant, and you will be released and can go to your home.'

'It is easy for you to talk,' said Aksyónof, 'but I have suffered for you these twenty-six years. Where could I go to now? . . . My wife is dead, and my children have forgotten me. I have nowhere to go. . . .'

Makár Semyónitch did not rise, but beat his head on the floor. 'Iván Dmítritch, forgive me!' he cried. 'When they flogged me with the knout it was not so hard to bear as it is to see you now . . . yet you had pity on me, and did not tell. For Christ's sake forgive me, wretch that I am!' And he began to sob.

When Aksyónof heard him sobbing he, too, began to weep.

'God will forgive you!' said he. 'Maybe I am a hundred times worse than you.' And at these words his heart grew light, and the longing for home left him. He no longer had any desire to leave the prison, but only hoped for his last hour to come.

In spite of what Aksyónof had said, Makár Semyónitch confessed his guilt. But when the order for his release came, Aksyónof was already dead.

(Written in 1872)

STORY 7

THE HAPPY PRINCE

Oscar Wilde

High above the city, on a tall column, stood the statue of the Happy Prince. He was gilded all over with thin leaves of fine gold, for eyes he had two bright sapphires, and a large red ruby glowed on his sword-hilt.

He was very much admired indeed. "He is as beautiful as a weathercock," remarked one of the Town Councillors who wished to gain a reputation for having artistic tastes; "only not quite so useful," he added, fearing lest people should think him unpractical, which he really was not.

"Why can't you be like the Happy Prince?" asked a sensible mother of her little boy who was crying for the moon. "The Happy Prince never dreams of crying for anything."

"I am glad there is someone in the world who is quite happy," muttered a disappointed man as he gazed at the wonderful statue.

"He looks just like an angel," said the Charity Children as they came out of the cathedral in their bright scarlet cloaks and their clean white pinafores.

"How do you know?" said the Mathematical Master, "you have never seen one."

"Ah! But we have, in our dreams," answered the children; and the Mathematical Master frowned and looked very severe, for he did not approve of children dreaming.

One night there flew over the city a little Swallow. His friends had gone away to Egypt six weeks before, but he had stayed behind, for he was in love with the most beautiful Reed. He had met her early in the spring as he was flying down the river after a big yellow moth, and had been so attracted by her slender waist that he had stopped to talk to her.

"Shall I love you?" said the Swallow, who liked to come to the point at once, and the Reed made him a low bow. So he flew round and round her, touching the water with his wings, and making silver ripples. This was his courtship, and it lasted all through the summer.

"It is a ridiculous attachment," twittered the other Swallows; "she has no money, and far too many relations"; and indeed the river was quite full of Reeds. Then, when the autumn came they all flew away.

After they had gone he felt lonely, and began to tire of his lady-love. "She has no conversation," he said, "and I am afraid that she is a coquette, for she is always flirting with the wind." And certainly, whenever the wind blew, the Reed made the most graceful curtseys. "I admit that she is domestic," he continued, "but I love travelling, and my wife, consequently, should love travelling also."

"Will you come away with me?" he said finally to her; but the Reed shook her head, she was so attached to her home.

"You have been trifling with me," he cried. "I am off to the Pyramids. Good-bye!" and he flew away.

All day long he flew, and at night-time he arrived at the city. "Where shall I put up?" he said; "I hope the town has made preparations."

Then he saw the statue on the tall column.

"I will put up there," he cried; "it is a fine position, with plenty of fresh air." So he alighted just between the feet of the Happy Prince.

"I have a golden bedroom," he said softly to himself as he looked round, and he prepared to go to sleep; but just as he was putting his head under his wing a large drop of water fell on him. "What a curious thing!" he cried; "there is not a single cloud in the sky, the stars are quite clear and bright, and yet it is raining. The climate in the north of Europe is really dreadful. The Reed used to like the rain, but that was merely her selfishness."

Then another drop fell.

"What is the use of a statue if it cannot keep the rain off?" he said; "I must look for a good chimney-pot," and he determined to fly away.

But before he had opened his wings, a third drop fell, and he looked up, and saw—Ah! What did he see?

The eyes of the Happy Prince were filled with tears, and tears were running down his golden cheeks. His face was so beautiful in the moonlight that the little Swallow was filled with pity.

"Who are you?" he said.

"I am the Happy Prince."

"Why are you weeping then?" asked the Swallow; "you have quite drenched me."

"When I was alive and had a human heart," answered the statue, "I did not know what tears were, for I lived in the Palace of Sans-Souci, where sorrow is not allowed to enter. In the daytime I played with my companions in the garden, and in the evening I led the dance in the Great Hall. Round the garden ran a very lofty wall, but I never cared to ask what lay beyond it, everything about me was so beautiful. My courtiers called me the Happy Prince, and happy indeed I was, if pleasure be happiness. So I lived, and so I died. And now that I am dead they have set me up here so high that I can see all the ugliness and all the misery of my city, and though my heart is made of lead yet I cannot chose but weep."

"What! Is he not solid gold?" said the Swallow to himself. He was too polite to make any personal remarks out loud.

"Far away," continued the statue in a low musical voice, "far away in a little street there is a poor house. One of the windows is open, and through it I can see a woman seated at a table. Her face is thin and worn, and she has coarse, red hands, all pricked by the needle, for she is a seamstress. She is embroidering passion-flowers on a satin gown for the loveliest of the Queen's maids-of-honour to wear at the next Court-ball. In a bed in the corner of the room her little boy is lying ill. He has a fever, and is asking for oranges. His mother has nothing to give him but river water, so he is crying. Swallow, Swallow, little Swallow, will you not bring her the ruby out of my sword-hilt? My feet are fastened to this pedestal and I cannot move."

"I am waited for in Egypt," said the Swallow. "My friends are flying up and down the Nile, and talking to the large lotus-flowers. Soon they will go to sleep in the tomb of the great King. The King is there himself in his painted coffin. He is wrapped in yellow linen, and embalmed with spices. Round his neck is a chain of pale green jade, and his hands are like withered leaves."

"Swallow, Swallow, little Swallow," said the Prince, "will you not stay with me for one night, and be my messenger? The boy is so thirsty, and the mother so sad."

"I don't think I like boys," answered the Swallow. "Last summer, when I was staying on the river, there were two rude boys, the miller's sons, who were always throwing stones at me. They never hit me, of course; we swallows fly far too well for that, and besides, I come of a family famous for its agility; but still, it was a mark of disrespect."

But the Happy Prince looked so sad that the little Swallow was sorry. "It is very cold here," he said; "but I will stay with you for one night, and be your messenger."

"Thank you, little Swallow," said the Prince.

So the Swallow picked out the great ruby from the Prince's sword, and flew away with it in his beak over the roofs of the town.

He passed by the cathedral tower, where the white marble angels were sculptured. He passed by the palace and heard the sound of dancing. A beautiful girl came out on the balcony with her lover. "How wonderful the stars are," he said to her, "and how wonderful is the power of love!"

"I hope my dress will be ready in time for the State-ball," she answered; "I have ordered passion-flowers to be embroidered on it; but the seamstresses are so lazy."

He passed over the river, and saw the lanterns hanging to the masts of the ships. He passed over the Ghetto, and saw the old Jews bargaining with each other, and weighing out money in copper scales. At last he came to the poor house and looked in. The boy was tossing feverishly on his bed, and the mother had fallen asleep, she was so tired. In he hopped, and laid the great ruby on the table beside the woman's thimble. Then he flew gently round the bed, fanning the boy's forehead with his wings. "How cool I feel," said the boy, "I must be getting better"; and he sank into a delicious slumber.

Then the Swallow flew back to the Happy Prince, and told him what he had done. "It is curious," he remarked, "but I feel quite warm now, although it is so cold."

"That is because you have done a good action," said the Prince. And the little Swallow began to think, and then he fell asleep. Thinking always made him sleepy.

When day broke he flew down to the river and had a bath. "What a remarkable phenomenon," said the Professor of Ornithology as he was passing over the bridge. "A swallow in winter!" And he wrote a long letter about it to the local newspaper. Every one quoted it, it was full of so many words that they could not understand.

"To-night I go to Egypt," said the Swallow, and he was in high spirits at the prospect. He visited all the public monuments, and sat a long time on top of the church steeple. Wherever he went the Sparrows chirruped, and said to each other, "What a distinguished stranger!" so he enjoyed himself very much.

When the moon rose he flew back to the Happy Prince. "Have you any commissions for Egypt?" he cried; "I am just starting."

"Swallow, Swallow, little Swallow," said the Prince, "will you not stay with me one night longer?"

"I am waited for in Egypt," answered the Swallow. "To-morrow my friends will fly up to the Second Cataract. The river-horse couches there among the bulrushes, and on a great granite throne sits the God Memnon. All night long he watches the stars, and when the morning star shines he utters one cry of joy, and then he is silent. At noon the yellow lions come down to the water's edge to drink. They have eyes like green beryls, and their roar is louder than the roar of the cataract."

"Swallow, Swallow, little Swallow," said the Prince, "far away across the city I see a young man in a garret. He is leaning over a desk covered with papers, and in a tumbler by his side there is a bunch of withered violets. His hair is brown and crisp, and his lips are red as a pomegranate, and he has large and dreamy eyes. He is trying to finish a play for the Director of the Theatre, but he is too cold to write any more. There is no fire in the grate, and hunger has made him faint."

"I will wait with you one night longer," said the Swallow, who really had a good heart. "Shall I take him another ruby?"

"Alas! I have no ruby now," said the Prince; "my eyes are all that I have left. They are made of rare sapphires, which were brought out of India a thousand years ago. Pluck out one of them and take it to him. He will sell it to the jeweller, and buy food and firewood, and finish his play."

"Dear Prince," said the Swallow, "I cannot do that"; and he began to weep.

"Swallow, Swallow, little Swallow," said the Prince, "Do as I command you."

So the Swallow plucked out the Prince's eye, and flew away to the student's garret. It was easy enough to get in, as there was a hole in the roof. Through this he darted, and came into the room. The young man had his head buried in his hands, so he did not hear the flutter of the bird's wings, and when he looked up he found the beautiful sapphire lying on the withered violets.

"I am beginning to be appreciated," he cried; "this is from some great admirer. Now I can finish my play," and he looked quite happy.

The next day the Swallow flew down to the harbour. He sat on the mast of a large vessel and watched the sailors hauling big chests out of the hold with ropes. "Heave a-hoy!" they shouted as each chest came up. "I am going to Egypt"!

cried the Swallow, but nobody minded, and when the moon rose he flew back to the Happy Prince.

"I am come to bid you good-bye," he cried.

"Swallow, Swallow, little Swallow," said the Prince, "will you not stay with me one night longer?"

"It is winter," answered the Swallow, "and the chill snow will soon be here. In Egypt the sun is warm on the green palm-trees, and the crocodiles lie in the mud and look lazily about them. My companions are building a nest in the Temple of Baalbec, and the pink and white doves are watching them, and cooing to each other. Dear Prince, I must leave you, but I will never forget you, and next spring I will bring you back two beautiful jewels in place of those you have given away. The ruby shall be redder than a red rose, and the sapphire shall be as blue as the great sea."

"In the square below," said the Happy Prince, "there stands a little match-girl. She has let her matches fall in the gutter, and they are all spoiled. Her father will beat her if she does not bring home some money, and she is crying. She has no shoes or stockings, and her little head is bare. Pluck out my other eye, and give it to her, and her father will not beat her."

"I will stay with you one night longer," said the Swallow, "but I cannot pluck out your eye. You would be quite blind then."

"Swallow, Swallow, little Swallow," said the Prince, "Do as I command you."

So he plucked out the Prince's other eye, and darted down with it. He swooped past the match-girl, and slipped the jewel into the palm of her hand. "What a lovely bit of glass," cried the little girl; and she ran home, laughing.

Then the Swallow came back to the Prince. "You are blind now," he said, "so I will stay with you always."

"No, little Swallow," said the poor Prince, "you must go away to Egypt."

"I will stay with you always," said the Swallow, and he slept at the Prince's feet.

All the next day he sat on the Prince's shoulder, and told him stories of what he had seen in strange lands. He told him of the red ibises, who stand in long rows on the banks of the Nile, and catch gold-fish in their beaks; of the Sphinx, who is as old as the world itself, and lives in the desert, and knows everything; of the merchants, who walk slowly by the side of their camels, and carry amber beads in their hands; of the King of the Mountains of the Moon, who is as black as ebony, and worships a large crystal; of the great green snake that sleeps in a palm-tree, and has twenty priests to feed it with honey-cakes; and of the pygmies who sail over a big lake on large flat leaves, and are always at war with the butterflies.

"Dear little Swallow," said the Prince, "you tell me of marvellous things, but more marvellous than anything is the suffering of men and of women. There is no Mystery so great as Misery. Fly over my city, little Swallow, and tell me what you see there."

So the Swallow flew over the great city, and saw the rich making merry in their beautiful houses, while the beggars were sitting at the gates. He flew into dark lanes, and saw the white faces of starving children looking out listlessly at the black streets.

Under the archway of a bridge two little boys were lying in one another's arms to try and keep themselves warm. "How hungry we are!" they said. "You must not lie here," shouted the Watchman, and they wandered out into the rain.

Then he flew back and told the Prince what he had seen.

"I am covered with fine gold," said the Prince, "you must take it off, leaf by leaf, and give it to my poor; the living always think that gold can make them happy."

Leaf after leaf of the fine gold the Swallow picked off, till the Happy Prince looked quite dull and grey. Leaf after leaf of the fine gold he brought to the poor, and the children's faces grew rosier, and they laughed and played games in the street. "We have bread now!" they cried.

Then the snow came, and after the snow came the frost. The streets looked as if they were made of silver, they were so bright and glistening; long icicles like crystal daggers hung down from the eaves of the houses, everybody went about in furs, and the little boys wore scarlet caps and skated on the ice.

The poor little Swallow grew colder and colder, but he would not leave the Prince, he loved him too well. He picked up crumbs outside the baker's door when the baker was not looking and tried to keep himself warm by flapping his wings.

But at last he knew that he was going to die. He had just strength to fly up to the Prince's shoulder once more. "Good-bye, dear Prince!" he murmured, "Will you let me kiss your hand?"

"I am glad that you are going to Egypt at last, little Swallow," said the Prince, "you have stayed too long here; but you must kiss me on the lips, for I love you."

"It is not to Egypt that I am going," said the Swallow. "I am going to the House of Death. Death is the brother of Sleep, is he not?"

And he kissed the Happy Prince on the lips, and fell down dead at his feet.

At that moment a curious crack sounded inside the statue, as if something had broken. The fact is that the leaden heart had snapped right in two. It certainly was a dreadfully hard frost.

Early the next morning the Mayor was walking in the square below in company with the Town Councillors. As they passed the column he looked up at the statue: "Dear me! How shabby the Happy Prince looks!" he said.

"How shabby indeed!" cried the Town Councillors, who always agreed with the Mayor; and they went up to look at it.

"The ruby has fallen out of his sword, his eyes are gone, and he is golden no longer," said the Mayor in fact, "he is little better than a beggar!"

"Little better than a beggar," said the Town Councillors.

"And here is actually a dead bird at his feet!" continued the Mayor. "We must really issue a proclamation that birds are not to be allowed to die here." And the Town Clerk made a note of the suggestion.

So they pulled down the statue of the Happy Prince. "As he is no longer beautiful he is no longer useful," said the Art Professor at the University.

Then they melted the statue in a furnace, and the Mayor held a meeting of the Corporation to decide what was to be done with the metal. "We must have another statue, of course," he said, "and it shall be a statue of myself."

"Of myself," said each of the Town Councillors, and they quarrelled. When I last heard of them they were quarrelling still.

"What a strange thing!" said the overseer of the workmen at the foundry. "This broken lead heart will not melt in the furnace. We must throw it away." So they threw it on a dust-heap where the dead Swallow was also lying.

"Bring me the two most precious things in the city," said God to one of His Angels; and the Angel brought Him the leaden heart and the dead bird.

"You have rightly chosen," said God, "for in my garden of Paradise this little bird shall sing for evermore, and in my city of gold the Happy Prince shall praise me."

STORY 8

THE CABULIWALLAH

Rabindranath Tagore

My five-year old daughter Mini cannot live without chattering. I really believe that in all her life she has not wasted a minute in silence. Her mother is often vexed at this, and would like to stop her prattle, but I would not. For Mini to be quiet is unnatural, and I cannot bear it long. And so my own talk with her is always lively.

One morning, for instance, when I was in the midst of the seventeenth chapter of my new novel, my little Mini stole into the room, and putting her hand into mine, said: 'Father! Ramdayal, the door-keeper, calls a crow a krow! He doesn't know anything, does he?'

Before I could explain to her the difference between one language and another in this world, she had embarked on the full tide of another subject. 'What do you think, Father? Bhola says there is an elephant in the clouds, blowing water out of his trunk, and that is why it rains!'

And then, darting off anew, while I sat still, trying to think of some reply to this: 'Father! What relation is Mother to you?'

With a grave face I contrived to say: 'Go and play with Bhola, Mini! I am busy!'

The window of my room overlooks the road. The child had seated herself at my feet near my table, and was playing softly, drumming on her knees. I was hard at work on my seventeenth chapter, in which Pratap Singh, the hero, has just caught Kanchanlata, the heroine, in his arms, and is about to escape with her by the third-storey window of the castle, when suddenly Mini left her play, and ran to the window, crying: 'A Cabuliwallah! A Cabuliwallah!' And indeed, in the street below, there was a Cabuliwallah, walking slowly along. He wore the loose, soiled clothing of his people, and a tall turban; he carried a bag on his back, and boxes of grapes in his hand.

I cannot tell what my daughter's feelings were when she saw this man, but she began to call him loudly. 'Ah!' thought I; 'he will come in, and my seventeenth chapter will never be finished!' At that very moment the Cabuliwallah turned, and looked up at the child. When she saw this, she was overcome by terror, and running to her mother's protection, disappeared. She had a blind belief that inside the bag, which the big man carried, there were perhaps two or three other children like herself. The pedlar meanwhile entered my doorway and greeted me with a smile.

So precarious was the position of my hero and my heroine, that my first impulse was to stop and buy something, since Mini had called the man to the house. I made some small purchases, and we began to talk about Abdur Rahman, the Russians, the English, and the Frontier Policy.

As he was about to leave, he asked: 'And where is the little girl, sir?'

And then, thinking that Mini must get rid of her false fear, I had her brought out.

She stood by my chair, and looked at the Cabuliwallah and his bag. He offered her nuts and raisins, but she would not be tempted, and only clung closer to me, with all her doubts increased.

This was their first meeting.

A few mornings later, however, as I was leaving the house, I was startled to find Mini, seated on a bench near the door, laughing and talking, with the great Cabuliwallah at her feet. In all her life, it appeared, my small daughter had never found so patient a listener, save her father. And already the corner of her little sari was stuffed with almonds and raisins, the gift of her visitor. 'Why did you give her those?' I said, and taking out an eight-anna piece, I handed it to him. The man accepted the money without demur, and put it into his pocket.

Alas, on my return, an hour later, I found the unfortunate coin had made twice its own worth of trouble! For the Cabuliwallah had given it to Mini; and her mother, catching sight of the bright round object, had pounced on the child with: 'Where did you get that eight-anna piece?'

'The Cabuliwallah gave it me,' said Mini cheerfully.

'The Cabuliwallah gave it you!' cried her mother greatly shocked. 'O Mini! How could you take it from him?'

I entered at that moment, and saving her from impending disaster, proceeded to make my own inquiries.

It was not the first or the second time, I found, that the two had met. The Cabuliwallah had overcome the child's first terror by a judicious bribe of nuts and almonds, and the two were now great friends.

They had many quaint jokes, which amused them greatly. Mini would seat herself before him, look down on his gigantic frame in all her tiny dignity, and with her face rippling with laughter would begin:

'O Cabuliwallah! Cabuliwallah! What have you got in your bag?'

And he would reply, in the nasal accents of the mountaineer: 'An elephant!' Not much cause for merriment, perhaps; but how they both enjoyed the fun! And for me, this child's talk with a grown-up man had always in it something strangely fascinating.

Then the Cabuliwallah, not to be behindhand would take his turn: 'Well, little one, and when are you going to your father-in-law's house?'

Now nearly every small Bengali maiden had heard long ago about her father-in-law's house; but we were a little new-fangled, and had kept these things from our child, so that Mini at this question must have been a trifle bewildered. But she would not show it, and with ready tact replied: 'Are you going there?'

Amongst men of the Cabuliwallah's class, however, it is well known that the words father-in-law's house have a double meaning. It is a euphemism for jail, the place where we are well cared for, at no expense to ourselves. In this sense would the sturdy pedlar take my daughter's question. 'Oh,' he would say, shaking his fist at an invisible policeman, 'I will thrash my father-in-law!' Hearing this, and picturing the poor discomfited relative, Mini would go off into peals of laughter in which her formidable friend would join.

These were autumn mornings, the very time of year when kings of old went forth to conquest; and I, without stirring from my little corner in Calcutta, would let my mind wander over the whole world. At the very name of another country, my heart would go out to it, and at the sight of a foreigner in the streets, I would fall to weaving a network of dreams—the mountains, the glens, and the forests of his distant land, with his cottage in their midst, and the free and independent life, or far away wilds. Perhaps scenes of travel are conjured up before me and pass and re-pass in my imagination all the more vividly, because I lead an existence so like a vegetable that a call to travel would fall upon me like a thunder-bolt. In the presence of this Cabuliwallah, I was immediately transported to the foot of arid mountain peaks, with narrow little defiles twisting in and out amongst their towering heights. I could see the string of camels bearing the merchandise, and the company of turbaned merchants, some carrying their queer old firearms, and some their spears, journeying downward towards the plains. I could see—. But at some such point Mini's mother would intervene, and implore me to 'beware of that man'.

Mini's mother is unfortunately very timid. Whenever she hears a noise in the streets, or sees people coming towards the house, she always jumps to the conclusion that they are either thieves, or drunkards, or snakes, or tigers, or malaria, or cockroaches, or caterpillars. Even after all these years of experience, she is not able to overcome her terror. So she was full of doubts about the Cabuliwallah, and used to beg me to keep a watchful eye on him.

If I tried to laugh her fear gently away, she would turn round seriously, and ask me solemn questions:

Were children never kidnapped?

Was it not true that there was slavery in Cabul?

Was it so very absurd that this big man should be able to carry off a tiny child?

I urged that, though not impossible, it was very improbable. But this was not enough, and her dread persisted. But as it was a very vague dread, it did not seem right to forbid the man to the house, and the intimacy went on unchecked.

Once a year, in the middle of January, Rahman, the Cabuliwallah, used to return to his own country, and as the time approached, he would be very busy, going from house to house collecting his debts. This year, however, he could always find time to come and see Mini. It might have seemed to a stranger that there was some conspiracy between the two, for when he could not come in the morning, he would appear in the evening.

Even to me it was a little startling now and then, suddenly to surprise this tall, loose-garmented man laden with his bags, in the corner of a dark room; but when Mini ran in smiling, with her, 'O Cabuliwallah! Cabuliwallah!' and the two friends, so far apart in age, subsided into their old laughter and their old jokes, I felt reassured.

One morning, a few days before he had made up his mind to go, I was correcting proof-sheets in my study. The weather was chilly. Through the window the rays of the sun touched my feet, and the slight warmth was very welcome. It was nearly eight o'clock, and early pedestrians were returning home with their heads covered. Suddenly I heard an uproar in the street, and, looking out saw Rahman being led away bound between two policemen, and behind them a crowd of inquisitive boys. There were bloodstains on his clothes, and one of the policemen carried a knife. I hurried out, and stopping them, inquired what it all meant. Partly from one, partly from another, I gathered that a certain neighbour had owed the pedlar something for a Rampuri shawl, but had denied buying it, and that in the course of the quarrel Rahman had struck him. Now, in his excitement, the prisoner began calling his enemy all sorts of names, when suddenly in a verandah of my house appeared my little Mini, with her usual exclamation: 'O Cabuliwallah! Cabuliwallah!' Rahman's face lighted up as he turned to her. He had no bag under his arm today, so that she could not talk about the elephant with him. She therefore at once proceeded to the next question: 'Are you going to your father-in-law's house?' Rahman laughed and said: 'That is just where I am going, little one!' Then seeing that the reply did not amuse the child, he held up his fettered hands. 'Ah!' he said, 'I would have thrashed that old father-in-law, but my hands are bound!'

On a charge of murderous assault, Rahman was sentenced to several years' imprisonment.

Time passed, and he was forgotten. Our accustomed work in the accustomed place went on, and the thought of the once free mountaineer spending his years in prison seldom or never occurred to us. Even my light-hearted Mini, I am ashamed to say, forgot her old friend. New companions filled her life. As she grew older, she spent more of her time with girls. So much, indeed, did she spend with them that she came no more, as she used to do, to her father's room, so that I rarely had any opportunity of speaking to her.

Years had passed away. It was once more autumn, and we had made arrangements for our Mini's marriage. It was to take place during the Puja holidays. With Durga returning to Kailas, the light of our home also would depart to her husband's house, and leave her father's in shadow.

The morning was bright. After the rains, it seemed as though the air had been washed clean and the rays of the sun looked like pure gold. So bright were they, that they made even the sordid brick-walls of our Calcutta lanes radiant. Since early dawn the wedding-pipes had been sounding, and at each burst of sound my own heart throbbed. The wail of the tune, Bhairavi, seemed to intensify the pain I felt at the approaching separation. My Mini was to be married that night.

From early morning noise and bustle had pervaded the house. In the courtyard there was the canopy to be slung on its bamboo poles; there were chandeliers with their tinkling sound to be hung in each room and verandah. There was endless hurry and excitement. I was sitting in my study, looking through the accounts, when someone entered, saluting respectfully, and stood before me. It was Rahman, the Cabuliwallah. At first I did not recognise him. He carried no bag, his long hair was cut short and his old vigour seemed to have gone. But he smiled, and I knew him again.

'When did you come, Rahman?' I asked him.

'Last evening,' he said, 'I was released from jail.'

The words struck harshly upon my ears. I had never before talked with one who had wounded his fellow-man, and my heart shrank within itself when I realised this; for I felt that the day would have been better-omened had he not appeared.

'There are ceremonies going on,' I said, 'and I am busy. Perhaps you could come another day?'

He immediately turned to go; but as he reached the door he hesitated, and said, 'May I not see the little one, sir, for a moment?' It was his belief that Mini was still the same. He had pictured her running to him as she used to do, calling 'O Cabuliwallah! Cabuliwallah!' He had imagined too that they would laugh and talk together, just as of old. Indeed, in memory of former days, he had brought, carefully wrapped up in a paper, a few almonds and raisins and grapes, obtained somehow or other from a countryman; for what little money had, had gone.

I repeated: 'There is a ceremony in the house, and you will not be able to see anyone today.'

The man's face fell. He looked wistfully at me for a moment, then said, 'Good morning,' and went out.

I felt a little sorry, and would have called him back, but I found he was returning of his own accord. He came close up to me and held out his offerings with the words: 'I have brought these few things, sir, for the little one. Will you give them to her?'

I took them, and was going to pay him, but he caught my hand and said: 'You are very kind, sir! Keep me in your memory. Do not offer me money! You have a little girl: I too have one like her in my own home. I think of her, and bring this fruit to your child—not to make a profit for myself.'

Saying this, he put his hand inside his big loose robe, and brought out a small and dirty piece of paper. Unfolding it with great care, he smoothed it out with both hands on my table. It bore the impression of a little hand. Not a photograph. Not a drawing. Merely the impression of an ink-smeared hand laid flat on the paper. This touch of the hand of his own little daughter he had carried always next to his heart, as he had come year after year to Calcutta to sell his wares in the streets.

Tears came to my eyes. I forgot that he was a poor Cabuli fruit-seller, while I was—. But no, what was I more than he? He also was a father.

That impression of the hand of his little Parvati in her distant mountain home reminded me of my own little Mini.

I sent for Mini immediately from the inner apartment. Many difficulties were raised, but I swept them aside. Clad in the red silk of her wedding-day, with the sandal paste on her forehead, and adorned as a young bride, Mini came and stood modestly before me.

The Cabuliwallah seemed amazed at the apparition. He could not revive their old friendship. At last he smiled and said: 'Little one, are you going to your father-in-law's house?'

But Mini now understood the meaning of the word 'father-in-law', and she could not answer him as of old. She blushed at the question, and stood before him with her bride-like face bowed down.

I remembered the day when the Cabuliwallah and my Mini had first met, and I felt sad. When she had gone, Rahman, sighed deeply and sat down on the floor. The idea had suddenly come to him that his daughter too must have grown up, while he had been away so long, and that he would have to make friends anew with her also. Assuredly he would not find her as she was when he left her. And besides, what might not have happened to her in these eight years?

The marriage-pipes sounded, and the mild autumn sunlight streamed round us. But Rahman sat in the little Calcutta lane, and saw before him the barren mountains of Afghanistan.

I took out a currency-note, gave it to him, and said: 'Go back to your daughter, Rahman, in your own country, and may the happiness of your meeting bring good fortune to my child!'

Having made this present, I had to curtail some of the festivities. I could not have the electric lights I had intended, nor the military band, and the ladies of the house were despondent about it. But to me the wedding-feast was all the more brighter for the thought that in a distant land a long-lost father had met again his only child.

STORY 9

THE STORY OF MUHAMMAD DIN

Rudyard Kipling

Who is the happy man? He that sees in his own house at home, little children crowned with dust, leaping and falling and crying.

—Munichandra

Translated by Professor Peterson

The polo-ball was an old one, scarred, chipped, and dinted. It stood on the mantelpiece among the pipe-stems which Imam Din, *khidmatgar,* was cleaning for me.

"Does the Heaven-born want this ball?" said Imam Din deferentially.

The Heaven-born set no particular store by it; but of what use was a polo-ball to a *khidmatgar*?

"By Your Honour's favour, I have a little son. He has seen this ball and desires it to play with. I do not want it for myself."

No one would for an instant accuse portly old Imam Din of wanting to play with polo-balls. He carried out the battered thing into the verandah and there followed a hurricane of joyful squeaks, a patter of small feet, and the *thud-thud-thud* of the ball rolling along the ground. Evidently the little son had been waiting outside the door to secure his treasure. But how had he managed to see that polo-ball?

Next day, coming back from office half an hour earlier than usual, I was aware of a small figure in the dining-room—a tiny, plump figure in a ridiculously inadequate shirt which came, perhaps, halfway down the tubby stomach. It wandered around the room, thumb in mouth, crooning to itself as it took stock of the pictures. Undoubtedly this was the "little son".

He had no business in my room, of course; but was so deeply absorbed in his discoveries that he never noticed me in the doorway. I stepped into the room and startled him nearly into a fit. He sat down on the ground with a gasp. His eyes opened and his mouth followed suit. I knew what was coming, and fled, followed by a long, dry howl which reached the servants' quarters far more quickly than any command of mine had ever done. In ten seconds Imam Din was in the dining-room. Then despairing sobs arose, and I returned to find Imam Din admonishing the small sinner who was using most of his shirt as a handkerchief.

"This boy," said Imam Din judicially, "is a *budmash*—a big *budmash.* He will, without doubt, go to the *jail-khana* for his behaviour." Renewed yells from the penitent, and an elaborate apology to myself from Imam Din.

"Tell the baby," said I, "that the *Sahib* is not angry, and take him away." Imam Din conveyed my forgiveness to the offender, who had now gathered all his shirt round his neck, string wise, and the yell subsided into a sob. The two set off for the door. "His name," said Imam Din, as though the name were part of the crime, "is Muhammad Din, and he is a *budmash*." Freed from present danger, Muhammad Din turned round in his father's arms, and said gravely, "It is true that my name is Muhammad Din, *tahib*, but I am not a *budmash*. I am a *man*!"

From that day dated my acquaintance with Muhammad Din. Never again did he come into my dining-room, but on the neutral ground of the garden we greeted each other with much state, though our conversation was confined to "*Talaam, tahib*" from his side, and "*Salaam, Muhammad Din*" from mine. Daily on my return from office, the little white shirt and the fat little body used to rise from the shade of the creeper-covered trellis where they had been hid; and daily I checked my horse here, that my salutation might not be slurred over or given unseemly.

Muhammad Din never had any companions. He used to trot about the compound, in and out of the castor-oil bushes, on mysterious errands of his own. One day I stumbled upon some of his handiwork far down the grounds. He had half buried the polo-ball in dust, and stuck six shrivelled old marigold flowers in a circle round it. Outside that circle again was a rude square, traced out in bits of red brick alternating with fragments of broken china; the whole bounded by a little bank of dust. The water-man from the well-curb put in a plea for the small architect, saying that it was only the play of a baby and did not much disfigure my garden.

Heaven knows that I had no intention of touching the child's work then or later; but, that evening, a stroll through the garden brought me unawares full on it; so that I trampled, before I knew, marigold-heads, dust-bank, and fragments of broken soap-dish into confusion, past all hope of mending. Next morning, I came upon Muhammad Din crying softly to himself over the ruin I had wrought. Someone had cruelly told him that the *sahib* was very angry with him for spoiling the garden, and had scattered his rubbish, using bad language the while. Muhammad Din laboured for an hour at effacing every trace of the dustbank and pottery fragments, and it was with a tearful and apologetic face that he said, "*Talaam tahib,*" when I came home from office. A hasty inquiry resulted in Imam Din informing Muhammad Din that, by my singular favour, he was permitted to disport himself as he pleased. Whereat the child took heart and fell to tracing the ground-plan of an edifice which was to eclipse the marigold-poloball creation.

For some months the chubby little eccentricity revolved in his humble orbit among the castor-oil bushes and in the dust; always fashioning magnificent palaces from stale flowers thrown away by the bearer, smooth water-worn pebbles, bits of broken glass, and feathers pulled, I fancy, from my fowls—always alone, and always crooning to himself.

A gaily-spotted sea-shell was dropped one day close to the last of his little buildings; and I looked that Muhammad Din should build something more than ordinarily splendid on the strength of it. Nor was I disappointed. He meditated for the better part of an hour, and his crooning rose to a jubilant song. Then he began tracing in the dust. It would certainly be a wondrous palace, this one, for it was two yards long and a yard broad in ground-plan. But the palace was never completed.

Next day there was no Muhammad Din at the head of the carriage-drive, and no "*Talaam, tahib*" to welcome my return. I had grown accustomed to the greeting, and its omission troubled me. Next day Imam Din told me that the child was suffering slightly from fever and needed quinine. He got the medicine, and an English doctor.

"They have no stamina, these brats," said the doctor, as he left Imam Din's quarters.

A week later, though I would have given much to have avoided it, I met on the road to the Musalman burying-ground Imam Din, accompanied by one other friend, carrying in his arms, wrapped in a white cloth, all that was left of little Muhammad Din.

STORY 10

A HAUNTED HOUSE

Virginia Woolf

Whatever hour you woke there was a door shutting. From room to room they went, hand in hand, lifting here, opening there, making sure—a ghostly couple.

"Here we left it," she said. And he added, "Oh, but here too!" "It's upstairs," she murmured. "And in the garden," he whispered "Quietly," they said, "or we shall wake them."

But it wasn't that you woke us. Oh, no. "They're looking for it; they're drawing the curtain," one might say, and so read on a page or two. "Now they've found it," one would be certain, stopping the pencil on the margin. And then, tired of reading, one might rise and see for oneself, the house all empty, the doors standing open, only the wood pigeons bubbling with content and the hum of the threshing machine sounding from the farm. "What did I come in here for? What did I want to find?" My hands were empty. "Perhaps it's upstairs then?"

The apples were in the loft. And so down again, the garden still as ever, only the book had slipped into the grass.

But they had found it in the drawing room. Not that one could ever see them. The window panes reflected apples, reflected roses; all the leaves were green in the glass. If they moved in the drawing room, the apple only turned its yellow side. Yet, the moment after, if the door was opened, spread about the floor, hung upon the walls, pendant from the ceiling—what? My hands were empty. The shadow of a thrush crossed the carpet; from the deepest wells of silence the wood pigeon drew its bubble of sound. "Safe, safe, safe," the pulse of the house beat softly. "The treasure buried; the room..." the pulse stopped short. Oh, was that the buried treasure?

A moment later the light had faded. Out in the garden then? But the trees spun darkness for a wandering beam of sun. So fine, so rare, coolly sunk beneath the surface the beam I sought always burnt behind the glass. Death was the glass; death was between us; coming to the woman first, hundreds of years ago, leaving the house, sealing all the windows; the rooms were darkened. He left it, left her, went North, went East, saw the stars turned in the Southern sky; sought the house, found it dropped beneath the Downs. "Safe, safe, safe," the pulse of the house beat gladly. "The Treasure yours."

The wind roars up the avenue. Trees stoop and bend this way and that. Moonbeams splash and spill wildly in the rain. But the beam of the lamp falls straight from the window. The candle burns stiff and still. Wandering through the house, opening the windows, whispering not to wake us, the ghostly couple seek their joy.

"Here we slept," she says. And he adds, "Kisses without number." "Waking in the morning—" "Silver between the trees—" "Upstairs—" "In the garden—" "When summer came—" "In winter snowtime—" The doors go shutting far in the distance, gently knocking like the pulse of a heart.

Nearer they come; cease at the doorway. The wind falls, the rain slides silver down the glass. Our eyes darken; we hear no steps beside us; we see no lady spread her ghostly cloak. His hands shield the lantern. "Look," he breathes. "Sound asleep. Love upon their lips."

Stooping, holding their silver lamp above us, long they look and deeply. Long they pause. The wind drives straightly; the flame stoops slightly. Wild beams of moonlight cross both floor and wall, and, meeting, stain the faces bent; the faces pondering; the faces that search the sleepers and seek their hidden joy.

"Safe, safe, safe," the heart of the house beats proudly. "Long years—" he sighs. "Again you found me." "Here," she murmurs, "sleeping; in the garden reading; laughing, rolling apples in the loft. Here we left our treasure—" Stooping, their light lifts the lids upon my eyes. "Safe! safe! safe!" the pulse of the house beats wildly. Waking, I cry "Oh, is this your buried treasure? The light in the heart."

OTHER HARDBACK BOOKS

- Abraham Lincoln by Lord Charnwood
  Biographies/Leaders, ISBN: 9789387669147
- Alice's Adventures in Wonderland by Lewis Carroll
  Children's/Classics, ISBN: 9789387669055
- Awakened Imagination by Neville Goddard
  Religion & Spirituality, ISBN: 9789389157185
- Be What You Wish by Neville Goddard
  Mind, Body & Spirit, ISBN: 9789388118163
- Becoming a Writer by Dorothea Brande
  Self Help/General, ISBN: 9789389157192
- Believe in Yourself by Joseph Murphy
  Mind, Body & Spirit, ISBN: 9789388118439
- Black Beauty by Anna Sewell
  Children's/Classics, ISBN: 9789388118262
- Civilization and Its Discontents by Sigmund Freud
  Social Sciences/General, ISBN: 9789388118279
- Feeling is the Secret by Neville Goddard
  Religion & Spirituality, ISBN: 9789389157208
- Gravity by George Gamow
  Sciences/Physics, ISBN: 9789388118705
- Great Speeches of Abraham Lincoln by Abraham Lincoln
  History/United States, ISBN: 9789387669154
- How to Attract Money by Joseph Murphy
  Self Help/Success, ISBN: 9789388118446
- How to be Filled with the Holy Spirit by A.W. Tozer
  Religion/Christianity, ISBN: 9789389157215
- How to Develop Self-Confi. and Pub. Speaking by Dale Carnegie
  Mind, Body & Spirit, ISBN: 9789388118286

Search the book by its ISBN

OTHER HARDBACK BOOKS

- How to Enjoy Your Life and Your Job by Dale Carnegie
  Self Help/General, ISBN: 9789388118293
- How to Stop Worrying and Start Living by Dale Carnegie
  Mind, Body & Spirit, ISBN: 9789387669161
- How to Win Friends and Influence People by Dale Carnegie
  Self Help/General, ISBN: 9789387669178
- Illust. Biography of William Shakespeare by Manju Gupta
  Biographies/Authors, ISBN: 9789387669246
- Madhubala by Manju Gupta
  Biographies/Cinems, ISBN: 9789387669253
- Meditations by Marcus Aurelius
  Non Fiction/Philosopy, ISBN: 9789388118781
- Mein Kampf by Adolf Hitler
  Autobiographies/Leaders, ISBN: 9789387669260
- My Experiments with Truth by Mahatma Gandhi
  Autobiographies/Leaders, ISBN: 9789387669277
- My Inventions: The Autobio. of Nikola Tesla by Nikola Tesla
  Autobiographies/Scientists, ISBN: 9789388118187
- Relativity by Albert Einstein
  Sciences/Physics, ISBN: 9789387669185
- Sense and Sensibility by Jane Austen
  Fiction/Classics, ISBN: 9789387669109
- The Alchemy of Happiness by Al-Ghazzali
  Religion & Spirituality, ISBN: 9789388118309
- The Art of Public Speaking by Dale Carnegie
  Self Help/General, ISBN: 9789388118477
- The Art of War by Sun Tzu
  Self Help/Success, ISBN: 9789387669321

Search the book by its ISBN

OTHER HARDBACK BOOKS

- The Autobiography of a Yogi by Paramahansa Yogananda
  Autobiographies/General, ISBN: 9789387669192
- The Diary of a Young Girl by Anne Frank
  Autobiographies/Memoirs, ISBN: 9789387669208
- The Dynamic Laws of Prosperity by Catherine Ponder
  Mind, Body & Spirit, ISBN: 9789388118194
- The Elements of Style by William Strunk
  Non Fiction/Skill, ISBN: 9789389157222
- The Game of Life and How to Play It by Florence Scovel Shinn
  Mind, Body & Spirit, ISBN: 9789388118316
- The Imitation of Christ by Thomas À Kempis
  Religion/Christianity, ISBN: 9789388118200
- The Knowledge of the Holy by A.W. Tozer
  Religion/Christianity, ISBN: 9789389157239
- The Magic of Believing by Claudie Bristol
  Religion/Christianity, ISBN: 9789388118217
- The Magic of Faith by Joseph Murphy
  Mind, Body & Spirit, ISBN: 9789388118712
- The Miracles of Your Mind by Joseph Murphy
  Mind, Body & Spirit, ISBN: 9789387669215
- The Origin of Species by Charles Darwin
  Sciences/Life Sciences, ISBN: 9789387669345
- The Path of Prosperity by James Allen
  Mind, Body & Spirit, ISBN: 9789388118323
- The Power of Awareness by Neville Goddard
  Mind, Body & Spirit, ISBN: 9789388118330
- The Power of Concentration by Theron Q. Dumont
  Self Help/General, ISBN: 9789388118224

Search the book by its ISBN

OTHER HARDBACK BOOKS

- The Power of Positive Thinking by Norman Vincent Peale
  Mind, Body & Spirit, ISBN: 9789388118729
- The Power of Your Subconscious Mind by Joseph Murphy
  Mind, Body & Spirit, ISBN: 9789387669222
- The Psychopathology of Everyday Life by Sigmund Freud
  Non Fiction/Psychology, ISBN: 9789388118231
- The Pursuit of God by A.W. Tozer
  Religion/Christianity, ISBN: 9789389157246
- The Quick and Easy Way to Effec. Speaking by Dale Carnegie
  Self Help/General, ISBN: 9789388118347
- The Richest Man in Babylon by George S. Clason
  Business & Economics, ISBN: 9789388118354
- The Science of Getting Rich by Wallace D. Wattles
  Self Help/Success, ISBN: 9789387669239
- The Seven Laws of Teaching by John Milton Gregory
  Self Help/General, ISBN: 9789388118460
- The Upanishads by Swami Paramananda
  Religion/Hinduism, ISBN: 9789388118774
- The World as I See It by Albert Einstein
  Non Fiction/Philosopy, ISBN: 9789388118248
- Think and Grow Rich by Napoleon Hill
  Self Help/Success, ISBN: 9789387669352
- Thought Vibration by William Walker Atkinson
  Non Fiction/Philosopy, ISBN: 9789389157253
- Wake Up and Live! by Dorothea Brande
  Mind, Body & Spirit, ISBN: 9789388118255
- Your Faith is Your Fortune by Neville Goddard
  Religion & Spirituality, ISBN: 9789389157260

Search the book by its ISBN